The Nehemiah Project

By R. A. Stokes

MountainFirePress

To Jesus Christ, my Lord and Savior: Thank You, Lord, for putting this story on my heart. May this book serve to further Your kingdom and glorify Your name.

To Mary Jo—my wife, companion, and friend: Thank you for your many years of love, friendship, and support.

So the wall was completed on the twenty-fifth of the month Elul, in fifty-two days. And it came about when all our enemies heard of it, and all the nations surrounding us saw it, they lost their confidence; for they recognized that this work had been accomplished with the help of our God.

Nehemiah 6:15-16 NASB

Note to the Reader

Have you ever wondered why there are so many Christian denominations? Certainly, there is biblical exhortation for unity among believers, yet doctrinal distinctives and oftentimes other divisions exist within the church.

Under the inspiration of the Holy Spirit, Paul tells us in 1 Corinthians 1:10, "Now I exhort you, brethren, by the name of our Lord Jesus Christ, that you all agree, and there be no divisions among you, but you be made complete in the same mind and in the same judgment" (NASB). In the Gospel of John, Jesus prayed, "that they all may be one, as You, Father, are in Me, and I in You; that they also may be one in Us, that the world may believe that You sent Me" (John 17:21 NKJV).

Within Christendom, we understand that doctrinal creeds based on Scripture are critical aspects of what we believe. We recognize that there are certain nonnegotiable distinctives that distinguish true Christianity from cults. Yet how many churchgoers blindly accepted the teachings of liberal denominations without ever seeking true counsel from the Word of God? We must all follow the example of the Bereans, who we read about in Acts: "Now these were more noble-minded than those in Thessalonica, for they received the word with great eagerness, examining the Scriptures daily, to see whether these things were so" (Acts 17:11 NASB).

Those who reverence the Bible as the living, breathing Word of God, who acknowledge Scripture as divinely inspired by the Holy Spirit, disagree on some scriptural passages, but we must never lose sight of the fact that through His Word, the Holy Spirit quickens our hearts and leads us into all truth. Neither one mortal man nor one denomination (and certainly not a figurehead in a fictional story) should ever be the sole reason a Christian believes what he or she may believe. Rather, as the Bible says in 2 Timothy, "Be diligent to present yourself approved to God as a workman who does not need to be ashamed, handling accurately the word of truth" (2 Timothy 2:15 NASB). Paul writes, "For as many as are led by the Spirit of God, they are the sons of God" (Romans 8:14).

At times in life, genuine Christians struggle with worldly distractions, doubts, fears, temptations, and dis-couragement, but true believers in Christ *should* be able to unite and come together to pray for revival. And, with God's help, believers *can* labor together on behalf of the King!

Chapter One

Benjamin Sharon—Sharon, as in Ariel Sharon, the prime minister of Israel, not Sharon, as in perhaps the name of your sister or your cousin or your next-door neighbor—was an unlikely arrival to this high-altitude, western mountains of New Mexico town, having lived most of his life in New York City. Staten Island, Brooklyn, Queens, the Bronx, and Manhattan—*yes*, all five boroughs in an unusually patterned succession of moves, each stay lasting between three and four years and corresponding symmetrically to his father's transfer from one synagogue to the next, one borough after the other, until the final borough, Manhattan, which represented no longer living under his father's domain, but rather, now, for the first time in his life, being independent as he always thought that he should be.

His father was a rabbi, and his father's father a rabbi as well, as were his father's brother and, it seemed, most of his father's friends—which only made sense years later when Benjamin understood that his father, Isaac Sharon, was not only the rabbi in his own synagogue but was also a Sanhedrin, a rabbi of rabbis, as well as an author, a lecturer, and a friend of everyone, or so Benjamin thought, who was reverent and devout and of importance within that sphere of spiritual influence.

This background—this Jewish pedigree of rabbinical thought and influence and traditional orthodox behavior and expectations, in really all manners of life, not simply in respect to Judaism and a culture that lived and breathed Jewish orthodoxy—of being a son in a long line of rabbinical tradition, made Benjamin's departure from the lineage that he was expected to remain in not simply alarming but also heretical in scope. It had been assumed he would be a rabbi ever since his birth, and there had never been even as much as a mention of his being anything else in life. And why should there be? What other vocation or "calling" could possibly have even a semblance of the importance of that of rabbi, which his father and his father's father before him had been obedient to?

But if that departure were not enough to create turmoil with his father—Isaac was a firm man of unflinching conviction, who, once convinced of the rightness of a given action, would proceed with an enviable manner of determination and vision and had no acceptance or tolerance for anyone's position that did not agree with his—there was something else about Benjamin's life that had become not simply intolerable but unforgivable. Benjamin had become a Christian! A Christian who, in a dramatic moment of conversion, had literally run up the aisle of the small nondenominational church he had attended for the first and only time and then submitted his life with finality to the kingship and lordship of Jesus Christ.

He initially did not understand the power he felt upon his life that night, but he did know that it was real. When the preacher had described the sacrifice of Jesus on the cross of Calvary—how God Almighty Himself had, incarnate, come into this life and been born of a virgin, lived a life among men, healed the sick, raised the dead, and yes, the absolute pinnacle of power, forgive sins, but then be crucified, rise again on the third day, descend into hell and proclaim the victory and then ascend into heaven and sit at the right hand of the Father—yes, a million times, yes, Benjamin was, in that moment, certain that Jesus was the promised Messiah, Yeshua, the One foretold through the centuries, the One his father and father before him still awaited.

This certainty did not come from an earnest and faithful study of the Holy Scriptures—that would come later. But as Benjamin had shared on many occasions since that evening, "The Holy Spirit came upon me in great magnitude. Although I knew little of Christianity beyond the Christmas holiday packaging of songs and gifts and ornaments and trees, and what I had been exposed to from a distance in school (many of my friends were 'Christian' but not necessarily 'born-again Christians'), I knew that evening that God was speaking to me and that what He was saying about Jesus, the promised Messiah, was true."

Alexander Joseph was both a mentor to and a protégé of Benjamin Sharon. A mentor, certainly, by way of years; Alexander was seventy-one, Benjamin fifty-two. A mentor as well because Alexander frequently counseled, encouraged, and yes, admonished Benjamin to stay the course that God had most definitely placed Benjamin on.

A protégé in that Benjamin's intense passion for revival, and the leadership that he provided the group, substantiated and validated the virtually equal desire held by Alexander to see a great move of the Holy Spirit among the people of Mountain Fire. It was one thing to teach about revival, as Alexander did in the religion class he taught at the local college, utilizing his professorship as a pulpit to describe and expound on historical revivals, all the while developing a platform for his vision of the revival that would happen here. It was quite another thing to organize the pastoral leadership and churches in such a way as to expedite that revival by bringing the people together to seek the Lord's face for a powerful move of God: this was Benjamin's gift from the Lord.

The ability to bring the pastors and lay people together to pray and seek God's face, the ability to persuade Christian leaders to put aside doctrinal distinctions and join together to labor for the advancement of the kingdom of God—this was a work that the Lord had entrusted to Benjamin, a work that most of Benjamin's peers could not do, a work that Alexander himself could not do.

Only Jesus could give Benjamin such favor, Alexander thought. So he too, after longing for revival for so many years, would follow Benjamin's vision, even in spite of the seemingly impossible obstacles.

Seven from the group were pastors: One of the men was a conservative Lutheran; two were Pentecostals; Compton had come out of the Holiness Methodist Movement; Gary was a Freewill Baptist; Jacob pastored an Evangelical Free church; Robert was a former missionary. One was a worship leader, one a businessman, one a professor/writer/speaker.

Jacob Randall and his twin brother, Justin, were from Iowa. Jacob pastored the Evangelical Free church; Justin led the worship team.

Robert Thompson pastored Grace Covenant Presbyterian after returning from mission work in South America for much of the last ten years.

The conservative Freewill Baptist mission organization had a strong presence on the Navajo reservation, and it was through this work that Gary had come to pastor Faith Bible Church.

Fire and brimstone were frequent themes of the Jesus Saves Pentecostal church led by Nathanial Allan. He was from Mississippi, by way of Alabama he always said, apparently meaning that in a positive way as he intimated that Mississippi had provided a platform of learning; Alabama had provided the means to carry that instruction out.

Then he would reverse the compliment by saying, "I

learned to talk in Mississippi. I learned to walk by faith in Alabama."

David Janssen's parsonage sat directly next to Elim Lutheran, a church affiliated with the Wisconsin Synod diocese. Here David lived with his wife, Elisha, and their six-year-old daughter. At age thirty-five, David was the youngest of the group.

Compton Atherton presided over a conservative Methodist congregation. The Holiness Methodist Movement had its roots in the Wesleyan Revival of 1730, which spread through America and England and contributed to much of the social reform the church had previously neglected.

Working from his home, Jack Broholm was a business consultant for Equity Resources, a division of Capital Growth Management (CGM) in Phoenix. His job was to market commercial loan refinancing projects, as well as to define, implement, and develop business models for small businesses in Arizona, Utah, New Mexico, Colorado, and Texas.

Faith Gospel Tabernacle, with a Foursquare Gospel affiliation, was the largest church within a sixty-mile radius, having a regular attendance on Sunday morning, and remarkably on Wednesday night as well, of five to six hundred. This was the church that Benjamin Sharon pastored. This was the church that Alexander Joseph and Jack Broholm attended.

High in the western mountains of New Mexico, nestled in the midst of surrounding red rocks, mesas, the jagged ridges of hogbacks, and foothills, sits the town of Mountain Fire.

At a high point of 6,830 feet altitude, the city of thirty thousand sits west of the Continental Divide, north of the Zuni Mountains, southwest of the Sangre de Cristo Mountain range, and east of the Arizona line. At one time the area was home to mountaineers, hunters, fur traders, gold seekers, riflemen, and bandits. By the early nineteen hundreds it was a railroad and mining town, in the '50s and '60s, a tourist stop on old U.S. Highway 66 on the stretch of road between San Bernardino and Chicago. Today, the fur traders are replaced by pawn shops and Indian jewelry merchants. A city largely populated by Native Americans and Hispanics, it was a melting pot of immigrants, mixing ideas, commerce, nationalities, and religions from other parts of the nation—yes, even other parts of the world.

And this is where, for a variety of reasons, the men had come—from virtually all over the country. "Exiled," as Benjamin liked to tell his congregation; "banished to," as Compton would say—each delineating the meaning of "how in the world did I end up here?" or, in a serious moment, "why did the Lord lead me to this place?"

And so there were ten.

Chapter Two

The gunshot, the glass shattering, the cashier's scream, and the man—who Benjamin would later learn was an agent with ISD in Houston—who yelled, "Hit the ground," had created such a deafening sound in such rapid succession that Benjamin had, almost instantly and subconsciously, entered a semi-dream state that he had experienced only once before. The instantaneousness of the events, the total surprise, and yes, to his dismay, the unforeseen prospect of this happening had placed Benjamin in as close to a state of shock as he thought possible.

He had just placed his billfold into the inside pocket of his overcoat when, in an instant, he saw the gun raised, the man by the pay phone undercut the Palestinian man's arm, the cashier raise her hands and scream, "No, don't do it," and the swing door from the back room open to the thrust of another man who lunged at the Palestinian. Benjamin dove toward the man's legs, but the other men had already toppled him, with the first man from the pay phone now pressing his knee into the gunman's neck. The gun had been knocked to the floor, away from the group, and Benjamin moved toward it.

"Don't touch it!" the man from the back room shouted forcefully at Benjamin. A siren was blaring at the front of the store, and the store's alarm created a piercing wail in the otherwise quiet night. Benjamin prepared to leave, but an officer now at the scene said, "You'll need to stay and give a report."

It seemed like hours to Benjamin, but twenty minutes later in the cold November night, the two men had handcuffed the gunman, placed him in an unmarked car, and driven away. They had pulled the two policemen at the scene aside, held an intense, heated conversation, initiated one very brief phone call for the sake of the policemen, and then, in an almost surreal moment, the policemen had gotten into their cars and driven away.

Benjamin's eyes and the gunman's eyes met as Benjamin walked toward his car. It was a look of familiarity from the man. A deep and penetrating look that said, "I know you."

It's impossible, Benjamin thought.

As Benjamin drove away, he said aloud, "It's nothing."

His mind was still racing as he pulled into the driveway of his home. And then he remembered; following his testimony to the two police officers—during which time the ISD agents were questioning the gunman and as Benjamin was getting into his car—one of the agents had said, "Be careful, Mr. Sharon." The distance between his interview with the police and the detained gunman was at least fifty feet. He never heard my testimony, Benjamin thought, and yet he referred to me as "Mr. Sharon."

That Sunday, Benjamin preached an especially powerful sermon to his congregation at Faith Gospel Tabernacle. The anointing of God was upon him in a mighty way as he paced the platform and cried out to those in the assembly.

"We need to redeem the time and number our days."

Benjamin testified how God had spared his life from the gunman, and he expounded upon the uncertainty of life.

"You don't know what tomorrow will bring. The Bible says that life is like a vapor, here today and then gone. Today is the day of salvation. When you hear His voice, harden not your heart. Yeshua, Jesus, the Messiah is calling you. Receive the salvation that He offers."

Twenty-two people responded to the invitation to come forward and receive Jesus into their hearts as Lord and Savior. The elders of the church then took them to the upper room, a second-floor room where four men and three women had been praying throughout the service, worshipping Jesus, praying for the anointing of the Holy Spirit upon Benjamin, and praying that God would soften the hearts of those in the congregation. Here in the upper room, the twenty-two new converts would be instructed in matters of the faith and be led in a salvation prayer. A prayer that acknowledged their sinfulness before Almighty God, expressed their willingness to turn away from, to repent of their sins, and then, finally, to ask Jesus into their hearts and be filled with the Holy Spirit.

That afternoon, Benjamin spent an hour in prayer agonizing with the Lord about several matters—the gunman and the meaning behind what had happened, the Lord's direction for Faith Gospel Tabernacle, and, of increasing urgency to Benjamin, the Lord's direction for the group. How was Benjamin to proceed? What was the next step? The weekly prayer times had been powerful. Everyone had sensed the presence of the Lord. Recent months had seen weeping, confession, even deep anguish over sin among the men. One after the other, the pastors and laymen had cried out to God for a move of the Holy Spirit in their midst. Benjamin was greatly encouraged, but what did the Lord want him to do now?

And he had wrestled with the Lord for healing among his flock, the flock that God had entrusted to him, a people with incredible hurts and pains and fears that Benjamin found beyond understanding.

Most of the parishioners were Navajo, although there were Hispanics and Anglos as well.

Many of the Navajo people lived on the reservation. Some worked in Mountain Fire; others were unemployed.

Benjamin reflected on his visit to the Yazzie home earlier that month and the dramatic conversion of ninety-year-old Margaret Yazzie just days before she died.

He had gone to visit Maggie at the request of Alfred, a parishioner of Faith Gospel Tabernacle and a grandson of the old woman. They rode together in Alfred's truck, going north on Vietnam Veterans Memorial Highway 371, beyond Crownpoint and past the limestone effigies, before heading east on a gravel road for several miles to the Yazzie residence. Benjamin viewed the red mesas that stood dramatically to the south and to the east, creating a stark contrast to the trailers, small sheds, and dilapidated vehicles that sat in a cluster near the hogan that Maggie lived in.

The five-acre plot of land that the extended Yazzie family lived on contained a small livestock farm. Horses drank from a trough in a corral surrounded by small piñon and juniper trees, while a small flock of sheep grazed in a field behind the corral. Chickens roosted in a pen near a trailer that Alfred lived in with his wife and three boys.

A spotted dog with a lopped off tail chased the truck down the lane, barking furiously as it moved toward the passenger door that Benjamin prepared to exit. Alfred sprung from the driver's side and quickly grabbed the mutt and held its collar as Benjamin walked to the hogan entrance.

Light shone through the windows accentuating the brilliant colors of the Navajo rugs that spread across two wooden tables sitting on the dirt floor. Smoke worked its way through the crowned rooftop from the wood burning stove at the center of the six-sided room.

Benjamin sat in a chair that Alfred had placed just in front of the old woman and looked at her intently as he took her hands in his.

Louis Yazzie, known to be a medicine man, sat in a chair opposite his elderly aunt.

Benjamin was a handsome man with short, curly black hair and a smooth, almost svelte complexion to his face. His eyes and cheeks gave off a vigor that belied his soon to be fifty-three years.

"Maggie, I'm Pastor Sharon. Alfred asked me to come and talk to you today."

Alfred repeated the words in Navajo and the old woman nodded.

"I'm here to tell you about Yeshua, Jesus."

Louis Yazzie slid his chair toward the window and reached his hand to turn up the radio.

"No," Alfred said sternly. Louis stopped and leaned back in his chair.

"Yeshua is the Ancient of Days," Benjamin continued. "Diyin God to the Navajo. He created these mesas and the land of your ancestors. He's blessed you with long life."

Again, Alfred repeated the words in Navajo, and again, without looking up, the old woman nodded that she understood.

"But someday all of us must die. We must face our maker. We must give an account to Yeshua of our life on this earth and the sins we've committed."

Maggie shook her head and closed her eyes. Benjamin saw the fear on her face when she opened them and spoke.

"She says that she is not at peace. She is not ready to meet Him," Alfred said softly.

Benjamin leaned close to the old woman and gently

rubbed her hands.

"I'm here today to tell you how you can have peace, that Yeshua can set you free. You can then meet Him and not be afraid. But you must be willing to accept His sacrifice for your sins. He died on a cruel tree so that you and I could have eternal life.

"Does this make sense to you?"

Alfred, very slowly and deliberately, repeated Benjamin's words.

"Will He accept me?" she asked.

"He will accept you if you are covered in His blood. But you must receive Him. You must accept the sacrifice He made for you. Will you do that right now?"

Maggie began to nod but stopped abruptly as she glanced at Louis. He was scowling and a low guttural sound emitted from his throat.

Benjamin took hold of Alfred's arm. "I'm going to pray, Alfred. Agree with me, brother."

Benjamin suddenly sprang to his feet and began praying in a strong, firm voice, "Yeshua, Your Word says that greater is He that is in us than he that is in the world. Your Word tells us that when the enemy comes in like a flood, You will raise up a standard against him.

"I ask You, in the mighty name of Yeshua Mashiach, Jesus Christ, to push back the darkness and send angels to surround this hogan and stand guard in this place. Spirit of darkness, Satan, I command you in the name of Yeshua to flee this home."

Louis Yazzie stood and walked to the door, cursing

under his breath. "I'll wait outside," he said.

A calm came over the old woman. "I want to be set free," Maggie replied.

Benjamin sat down and placed his hand on Maggie's head. "I want to lead you in a prayer. You must mean every word that you say."

Phrase by phrase, Benjamin prayed, confessing sin, acknowledging Yeshua's death at Calvary and His atoning blood for all who will accept Him, expressing a willingness to turn from the sins of the past and to follow Jesus for as many or as few days as the old woman might have left.

With each sentence, Alfred repeated the words in Navajo; with each sentence, Maggie repeated the words.

With tears streaming down her face, the old woman closed her prayer with Benjamin's final words. "I commit my life to you. I invite You, Lord Jesus, into my heart. Amen."

Maggie died three days later.

Chapter Three

Benjamin hadn't expected the level of confession that would accompany that Thursday's prayer meeting. All of the men were present as Jack Broholm began speaking. "Nine years ago I filed for bankruptcy protection for a business I was involved with. It so devastated my life that I virtually dropped out of ministry."

Robert Thompson followed. "I haven't tithed—actually for most of the years of my ministry. Not even to my own church. I was always worried about having enough for retirement. My salary was always adequate; the church met our needs financially. But the salary was never what I felt it should be. As a result, I rationalized that my service to the Lord and His flock compensated for my tithe. About a year ago the Lord dealt with me and convicted me of my sin."

"There isn't a week that goes by that I don't worry about the future," began Compton Atherton, echoing some of Robert's concerns. "I pore over my investments and savings, and there never seems to be enough. At times, my heart seems overwhelmed by the cares of this life. I loathe these thoughts of worldliness and self. Sometimes, I literally cry out to the Lord for help and mercy."

Justin confessed to being impatient with his wife and kids, and failing to be the husband and father the Lord required of him.

Jacob confessed to loneliness and failing to trust in the Lord. "I often look to myself, when I should have my eyes on Him."

Gary Smith confessed to an indifference at times to the needs of his people. "I lack love. Even those that respond to my altar calls have become numbers at times. I don't understand how my heart could be so cold."

"There is a pride in my preaching," Nathanial Allan began. "Not so much style and delivery, although that too, but primarily in speaking the truth. I always feel as if my messages are closer to the truth than everyone else's. I ask each of you to forgive me."

David Janssen had a despairing look about him. "I've been extremely judgmental for most of my Christian life. Oftentimes, I question the salvation of other professing believers." David lifted his eyes. "Have mercy on me, Lord."

And so they went, one by one.

Alexander spoke softly. "I've been a Christian since I was eleven years old. I've labored faithfully for sixty years. I've preached and taught the Word of God. I was a missionary for a time, and now I teach about revival at a college where most of the students, most of my students, are not believers—though they are invited into the kingdom frequently. I've come to not only expect revival in my lifetime—which has been my prayer—but also to feel that God owes me that revival."

Alexander looked down, saddened by the grief he felt he had caused the Lord. "The Lord doesn't owe me revival. I owe Him—everything."

"There's something I haven't told you," Benjamin said quietly. "There are five . . ."

Suddenly the men were interrupted by a loud cry from Compton Atherton. "Lord Jesus, forgive me. I'm a selfish man," he cried out. Within seconds he was sobbing and then fell to his knees.

Robert came across the circle, and as Atherton knelt, Robert leaned forward and embraced him.

Gary Smith, too, went to his knees. One after the other, the men dropped to the floor. Compton stretched prostrate weeping before the Lord. Benjamin laid his hand on Compton's shoulder and cried out, "Yeshua, Lord Jesus, Lamb of God. It says in Your Word that if we confess our sins, You are faithful and just to forgive us our sins. None of these sins today have taken You by surprise. In all eternity past, in the secret counsel of the Triune God, Elohay Selichot, You knew what would happen here today. And You still loved us and had mercy on us."

Alexander closed in prayer. "Father, may each of us fulfill our destinies—the divine destiny that You have laid before us. Whether that of health or sickness, affluence or poverty, comfort or hardship, clarity or testing, even, if You so desire, to allow trials and persecution, let us be faithful to Your plan. Let us be faithful to the great cause of Christ by laying down our lives as living sacrifices for You. I ask this in the blessed and mighty name of Jesus. Amen."

Chapter Four

Alexander Joseph lived and breathed the subject of revival. He studied the great historical revivals of Western civilization, such as the Great Awakening that occurred in the American colonies from 1730 to 1745, with the ensuing passion for holiness among God's people. He lectured on the Wesleyan-Whitefield revival that so greatly impacted continents on both sides of the Atlantic. He taught on the Second Great Awakening that took place less than one hundred years later, as the Holy Spirit anointed Charles Finney to begin preaching in western New York. He frequently referenced the Welsh Revival where the Lord raised up twenty-six-year-old Evan Roberts to travel from church to church admonishing the people to repent and turn to God. He taught on lesser-known moves of God as well, like the Hebrides Revival that occurred in the 1930s in the Hebrides Islands of Scotland and the Azusa Street Revival in Los Angeles early into the twentieth century—a precursor to the Assemblies of God breaking off from A.B. Simpson's

Missionary Alliance denomination and a forerunner to the modern-day Pentecostal Movement. He thoroughly documented his research, archiving his files in a library extensively devoted to great moves of God.

He shared detailed anecdotes with Benjamin and the other men. He spoke at six to eight conferences a year—traveling as far as Argentina on one occasion—and he wrote articles for several leading Christian publications. He taught classes about revival at local churches, he lectured about them at the college he worked at, and he spoke about them with his peers in an almost relentless manner.

Alexander was consumed with revival. And not simply with revivals of times past but in looking for a touch of God upon the lives of the people of Mountain Fire: a revival every bit as powerful, every bit as redemptive, and every bit as recognizable as the great revivals down through the ages.

There were certain characteristics that accompanied every revival he had studied and certain "ingredients" that Alexander deemed necessary—or, more importantly, that he felt God required before touching a certain people.

In his classroom the next morning, Alexander began his lecture by saying, "There are times that God anoints an entire group—such as the twelve disciples. But oftentimes throughout Scripture, He selects one man to 'lead the charge,' so to speak. He anoints one man for a particular time, a particular season. That is one of the most difficult things for church leaders to accept as they contemplate coming together to do a great work for the Lord. In other words, if you line up fifteen church leaders in a given area, for a given work, three or four of that group will want to be in charge. Three or four will want to lead the group, and in some instances, each of those men will believe that he is the one the Lord has chosen."

"So how will the group know which of the men has been appointed by the Lord?" a student asked.

"Typically," Alexander continued, "the man chosen will have a general favor with the group at large as far as consistency in his own ministry. He's maintained his ministry focus over a period of time. He also has the ability to move the work along. He will be a man devoted to prayer and, more often than not, a man who is consumed with evangelism. He will not be a 'four-walls' leader—a pastor who doesn't heed the call to 'Go ye into all the world, and preach the gospel to every creature' but instead ministers solely within the walls of his church. He will also not be the man who believes that the coming revival is selectively for his church only.

"The man who leads the local body of believers understands that the body of Christ is comprised of many different denominations and creeds. He will not try to exclusively elevate his own church. He will work to encompass as many of those groups as possible without compromising the salvation message of being saved 'by grace through faith.' The Lord will place a goal, a vision, on that pastor or layman's heart, and soon that vision will be so consuming as to engulf not simply the pastor but the group as well. He will be accountable to his peers, but first and foremost he will be accountable to the Lord."

Alexander paused. "A man like Benjamin Sharon.

"A man who realizes that it is not about him, that he's just an instrument in the Almighty's hand. And yet, a leader who understands that were he to refuse the call, God could simply appoint someone else in a like manner to the admonition that Mordecai gave Esther."

Alexander straightened up and waved his hand, pointing his forefinger upward. "Listen closely, class. Esther was given a mandate from God, but she was afraid. Mordecai told her that if she refused God's call, she would perish and that if she was disobedient, God would simply raise someone else up to fulfill His call."

"Can a man ever walk away from his calling without God filling the void?" a student asked.

"That's a very good question. If you mean, can a man walk away from his calling and leave a vacuum, without accomplishing the work God has given him and without God raising up a successor? then I would say no, I don't believe so. Benjamin Sharon, my pastor, would suggest otherwise."

Alexander smiled as Benjamin walked into the classroom and sat down in the last row.

"Pastor Sharon would say that God, in His divine providence and perfect will, had ordained that person for a specific task and that, in some instances, in the scope of free will, a man could walk away from his calling, leaving behind an unfulfilled destiny."

"Thank you, Alexander. I appreciate your eloquence in presenting my views. I would like to announce to the class that Professor Joseph has given you a preview this morning. I will be preaching on Esther chapter 4 at a special service in the coming weeks, and I encourage all of you to attend. Alexander will inform you of the details in the days ahead."

As the class ended and the students were leaving, Benjamin and Alexander embraced.

"I am surprised! What have I done to merit the honor of your visit this morning? What brings you here today, Benjamin?"

He looked intently at Benjamin, who was unshaven and appeared tired.

Benjamin sensed his friend's concern.

"I must tell you something of grave importance. I have not slept all night. Yeshua placed a vision on my heart last night. We're to call the body of Christ together for a special prayer meeting. We will assemble the people for a time of seeking Yeshua for His presence in our midst. I will announce it to the group when we meet on Thursday."

Alexander was ecstatic. Yes, he thought, of course. A prayer assembly for the people to come together and humble themselves before God. He could scarcely contain the exuberance he felt.

"The Holy Spirit came upon me with great force. Hour after hour through the night He spoke to my heart and impressed upon me a message for the people. He told me that He would visit the assembly and touch the people.

"There's much more. I will fill you in later. I need to rest. Keep me in prayer. Shalom, my friend."

With that, Benjamin left abruptly, and Alexander stood in the empty classroom and extended his arms to heaven. "Blessed be the name of the Lord," he cried aloud. His extended arms gave him a towering persona. His white beard and wavy gray and white hair gave him more than a professorial look. He had the appearance of a prophet of old. He looked somewhat like the man on the cover of Blackaby and King's *Experiencing God.*

The revival would come, Alexander thought. By God's grace he would see the hand of God in Mountain Fire.

Chapter Five

In addition to being a pastor, Benjamin Sharon was also a runner, having run USTAF marathons in twelve states as well as in London and Barcelona. He had endured Heartbreak Hill in Boston, set a PR (personal record) in Chicago, observed the smiles that transformed to somber stares when the spectators lining the streets of heavily Jewish populated New York City suddenly drew close enough to view and understand the words of his running sweatshirt, "King of kings and Lord of lords – JESUS," and raised his arms in jubilant exuberance after completing the Philadelphia Marathon on a cold, rainy November morning.

His goal was to become a member of the 50 States Marathon Club and ultimately run one marathon in all fifty states. But now, fast approaching fifty-three, and with twenty more pounds on his six-foot frame than during his primary running years, Benjamin was slowing down. He still ran regularly (or plodded along, as he often quipped)—two- to ten-mile runs through the neighborhood and out beyond the college in the outskirts of Mountain Fire—but the times were more for exercise and reflection than for speed. But even though the pace of his running had slowed, the conditioning was there; if time would permit, Benjamin could still, on short notice, enter a 26.2-mile marathon and run the entire race.

Sermons were frequented with endurance metaphors, and why not? Certainly the Christian walk was all about endurance, all about valleys and mountaintops, and all about finishing in victory.

Even as he cared for the sheep that Yeshua had entrusted to him, there was a special emphasis placed on developing and motivating leaders to a greater walk. "All of you men and women are unique," he would say. "Each of you have a special place of service set aside for great accomplishments in the Lord."

Benjamin's Orthodox Jewish upbringing made for some of the more pronounced differences within the group, but that aside, the personalities and theological stance held by each of the men made for an unlikely alliance.

Nathanial Allan was the most charismatic of the group, attracting attention, like honey to a comb, from virtually everyone he came in contact with—male, female; young, old; rich, poor.

Alexander always said that Nathanial looked and preached like Billy Sunday, only Billy was more subdued. Nathanial not only was all over the platform but up and down the aisles as well, stopping at any point in the message to suddenly lay hands upon a parishioner's head and pray for God's blessing on that person. And on one memorable Sunday, walking every aisle, eyes glaring, finally jumping on a table at the rear of the church and giving the altar call to a hushed congregation that felt their preacher's anger against sin.

He regularly preached a fiery message, only occasionally soothing a concerned soul by saying, "Don't be offended. I'm not talking to you. I'm talking to the person next to you."

Nathanial cherished Alexander's words. "Who wouldn't want to be compared to Billy Sunday?" he said. But even more than that he cherished the compliment that Benjamin had paid: "Your outreach efforts, my brother, put us all to shame."

Nathanial was a New Testament man, preaching physical, emotional, and spiritual healing from the Gospels and Epistles. "I love the Old Testament," he would say, "but the grace that abounds from Matthew to Revelation will keep me in the New Testament at least another five years."

Everyone said that he could have played pro ball. He was that good. But a calling had been on his life since he was five years old, and his mother had prophesied over him, saying, "You're going to be placed by God in a distant land and be used by the Almighty to usher souls into the kingdom." Since the age of twenty-one he had chased after that calling, taking hold of everything that God had for him.

Robert Thompson devoted half of his week to his Sunday morning sermon, five to ten hours to the Thursday night teaching sermon, and another hour on the Sunday evening prayer-time devotion. The congregation of about three hundred, consisting largely of members of the medical and teaching communities, was affluent enough to support an associate pastor as well as a minister of youth. These men tended to most of the counseling and support activities, leaving Robert to concentrate on what he felt his most important role was: feeding the flock with the Word of God.

Robert's memory was enviable if not phenomenal. During his sermons he rarely left the conservative safety of the lectern, but his engagement with his congregation was notable to say the least.

His preaching was very precise, rarely generalized, but rather, like a laser beam, he employed pinpoint phrasing in his messages. Robert believed that there was a specific purpose and resolve in everything that Jesus said and did. There was no wasted motion, but rather, everything was concise and intentional. But his analysis was not confined merely to efficiency. More importantly, there was no dominating thought of self. Jesus led a life of service that focused on obedience to the exact will of the Father.

Robert loved the flock that the Lord had entrusted to him. All of the children, from the time they were born and brought to church by their parents, were greeted by name, without fail, at the end of each service, as Robert stood in the foyer shaking hands, pinching cheeks, embracing friends. Young and old alike were acknowledged, remembered, and made to feel special. If a member missed more than one Sunday in a row, Robert was on the phone or sending a card. He had a pastor's heart that determined to include and maintain each of the sheep the Lord had given him.

Faith Bible was the smallest church in the group with a congregation of eighty-five—about half of whom attended church regularly. Gary Smith was a humble, quiet man. He had ministered now for thirty-five years—five in Mountain Fire—and, with the Lord's help, would continue as long as He would have him.

His father had been a pastor in Virginia until the age of seventy-five before finally leaving the pulpit, and only then to bury his wife, and shortly after that his brother. Joshua "Pete" Smith was the finest example of an earthly man Gary had ever seen. He was the kindest, never refusing a neighbor in need of anything, whether food, clothing, or money; he was the strongest, still chopping and hauling wood at seventy-five; and he was the most spiritual, still running the pews without missing a step right up to the last day that he preached. More than that: he knew his God as intimately as any man Gary had known. And then the Lord took him home too.

Gary would borrow from his father's notes, picking up nuggets of gold, nuggets of truth that were timeless in their power.

Gary also had the prison ministry in town, faithfully

giving an early Sunday morning message before arriving at Faith Bible Church and preaching to his own congregation.

Working from his home, Jack Broholm spent his time consulting with small businesses and seeking commercial real estate based refinancing projects in the $1 million to $5 million range. At one time he held a seat on the Chicago Board of Trade, buying and selling commodities. Trading futures contracts was exhilarating, rewarding, and as stressful as anything he had ever done. "A young man's job," Jack would say; a young man representing an investor with a large portfolio—one that could weather the occasional loss that accompanied the futures market.

David Janssen lived in an elaborate stone-wrought parish provided by the Wisconsin Lutheran synod. Elim Lutheran Church was a beautiful building situated on a hill at the highest point in Mountain Fire. The city sat in a valley surrounded by rock formations, mesas, and foothills, and the church offered breathtaking views from the vestibule, Sunday school rooms, and David's office. A narrow, winding staircase led to a high steeple with a one-hundred-year-old church bell that had been brought to Mountain Fire from Michigan when the church was established. David rang the church bell every Sunday morning at eight, as well as on special occasions throughout the year. David's wife played the pipe organ each Sunday morning, Sunday night, and Wednesday evening. The congregation was affluent and included several prominent business leaders from the area.

In a number of ways, Compton Atherton was the most unlikely member of the group. He was also the last pastor that Benjamin had asked to join the weekly prayer meeting. Benjamin prayed fervently that God would complete the alliance and He had. He pointed to Compton T. Atherton, pastor of the second largest church in Mountain Fire, a congregation of four hundred, mostly professional, largely of Anglo-Saxon, European descent, extremely conservative, and very much orthodox in their approach to worship. By appearances, Compton was a professional clergyman. He was an immaculate dresser, frequently donning three-piece suits, finely tailored with perfectly coordinated shirts, colorful ties, and shiny black shoes. His hair was combed back and parted in the middle, giving him a 1930s look. He had a dashing, Gatsby sort of air about him. Those that didn't know him well described him as arrogant and pious. But Compton loved the Lord and faithfully preached the gospel message to his congregation.

His sermons always started slowly, carefully articulating each word, each phrase—like Robert Thompson, never wasting words and with no wasted motion. But, in his own manner, like a finely tuned orchestra, Compton would end with a crescendo that seemed to shake the prism of stained glass in the sanctuary windows as if a dance had begun along the walls.

Compton never left the pulpit. He always preached Scripture; he always challenged the congregation with life-changing messages.

He also initially said no to Benjamin. But God convicted him of his own coldness and the coldness of his congregation. It wasn't enough to preach the gospel faithfully and then, in between, live his comfortable life oblivious to the needs around him, void of the compassion of Christ. Where was the concern over the lost? A concern manifested in giving all of himself to a world lost and perishing without the Savior? When was the last time he had wept over the lost?

Jacob Randall had enjoyed the acclaim of being a high school wrestling star—no small accomplishment in Iowa. He had wrestled at 150 like his collegiate heroes Nate Carr from Iowa State and Bruce Kinseth from Iowa. Jacob was taller than the stout Carr, wiry and closer in build to the lean Kinseth, and as fast on his feet as either.

His claim to fame in Iowa wrestling circles was "the dance," an electrifying, explosive, single-leg takedown in which his knees scarcely touched the mat, followed by immediately allowing his opponent to escape. And then the dance began: a frenzy of motion that left the opponent so off-balance that Jacob would literally go straight over the top, chest to chest, oftentimes consummating in a pin. It was a pleasure to watch—for the novice fan and wrestling purest alike.

His aspiration from the time he was ten years old was to wrestle for Dan Gable, but the closest he came was the Iowa Wrestling Camp two summers in a row in Iowa City. A knee injury following a high school state championship ended his dream of an NCAA gold.

It didn't seem right. He had hoped and prayed for his chance, his moment in the sun, and in one agonizing instant his hopes were ended. There really had not been anything else that mattered as far as pursuits in this life, and the depression that followed the death of his dream led way to a year of alcohol and drugs. The Lord had other plans, Jacob came to realize.

Justin Randall was a musical prodigy. While Jacob was wrestling, Justin was advancing a musical symphony—his life—that would be used by the Lord in ways he would not see until years later.

As a musician, he had perfect pitch. He took classical piano lessons from the time he was four. He learned trumpet and sax by listening to his parents' Herb Alpert & The Tijuana Brass record albums. When "Dueling Banjos" became a hit song, he learned both the guitar and banjo parts in a morning. He played percussion, wood, brass, and string.

As a worship leader, Justin played keyboards and sang. His tenor voice could reach three octaves.

His office walls were adorned with a collection of vintage musical instruments, hung symmetrically on two of the walls; a sparkling gold trumpet circa 1950s handed down from his father, a saxophone, clarinet, tambourine, cymbal, mandolin, violin, and the largest instrument—taking up considerable space on the wall facing him—a 1947 hollow body Gibson L-7, the F-holes making a stark contrast to the round center on his Martin acoustic that leaned against the wall.

But his prize was a gift from Benjamin, who had said, "There's a story behind this, my friend. A story, I'm afraid, that will have to wait for another day." He then handed Justin the shofar, which hung gracefully as a centerpiece in the room.

Alexander Joseph sat quietly in his church office and gazed momentarily out the window at the gray December sky. Alexander reflected on the age of the men in the group. Most were in their late forties or early fifties. He was the patriarch, the elder statesman.

They were at a good age, he felt—old enough to have the respect of the elderly, young enough to be taken seriously by the youth; the optimum leadership stage, he thought.

Alexander marveled at Benjamin's ability to focus on and accentuate the common bond the men shared in Christ while simultaneously downplaying the differences.

God was moving in a special way in Mountain Fire. The clouds of revival were forming.

The late afternoon sun shone brightly on Pyramid Rock and Church Rock, and the clouds cast shadows on the foothills in the forefront and the red mesas to the west as Benjamin began a twelve-mile run east of the college. He would gradually ascend five hundred feet as he wound toward Pine Lake four miles from the school. From there he would circle the lake and then descend to Mountain Fire.

As he ran, he thought of his father, Rabbi Sharon as everyone still referred to him, even after his death of ten years before. Benjamin had been estranged from his family since his conversion at twenty-six, scarcely speaking to his father for the last fifteen years he was alive.

He thought about his mother, who would call twice a month and who, in the early years whenever Rabbi Sharon was away, would listen politely to Benjamin's gospel presentation. She only called when her husband was gone, and upon his arrival, she would abruptly end the conversation. But in the meantime she would update Benjamin on his nephews and nieces and the rest of the family.

Benjamin's younger brother was an attorney in Manhattan. His law firm, which specialized in real estate closings—or at least that was as close to a description as Mrs. Sharon could ever come to—was flourishing. His sister had two boys and two girls, all of whom attended the separate boys' and girls' schools on Bedford Avenue in the Hasidic Jewish section of Williamsburg, Brooklyn.

And he thought of Sarai Levy and the life they might have had together.

He would never forget the expression of despair when he told her of his faith in Yeshua. Her rich, brown eyes looked as if she had lost everything, that nothing else mattered, that her life was over.

"You can't do this, Benjamin. Please, I beg you."

"You must believe," he told her. "What I'm telling you is true."

Sarai's father was a wealthy businessman who attended Rabbi Sharon's synagogue. He was a strong financier of various Israeli causes and had helped Benjamin with his mission. He knew people—"the right people," those who knew him would say. Once he became involved, things happened quickly. Where Rabbi Sharon provided a spiritual perspective of Israel, Mr. Levy provided a practical Zionist message, backed up with concerted efforts. "A house cannot prosper with enemies within," he would say. Mr. Levy supported right-wing, pro-Israeli groups that would not consider a Palestinian homeland within the established boundaries of Zion—boundaries established in 1948 by the international community and then again in 1967 at the hand of war. He regularly contributed funds to combat Fatah, the PLO, and other radical Palestinian splinter groups. "Let me give you an analogy," he would tell Benjamin. "If you are in business and someone is stealing from you, what do you do? You fire the person. You must understand—in reality, there is no peace plan. Don't you think that an individual who straps his back with explosives and kills innocent people maintains a greater commitment to his cause than a common thief whose presence is removed from a business? They must be expelled!"

He and Benjamin would talk for hours, Sarai sitting silently on the couch, leaning her head on Benjamin's shoulder.

For the time Benjamin was away, she would wait faithfully and write often. They would talk by phone at least weekly. She would visit annually, and he would be home for vacations.

They would marry in July, three months after he was back to stay.

She was an only child. The wedding would be the largest and most beautiful Jewish ceremony ever held in Congregation Beth Abraham, a synagogue in Brooklyn.

"Benjamin, Benjamin, sweet Benjamin. What have you done, my love?" Sarai leaned on his shoulder and wept softly.

It was over. Somehow instinctively, in these moments, they both knew that it could never be the same again.

They continued to see each other for several months, although clandestinely, because by now both families had distanced themselves from Benjamin. Sarai offered to leave with him and start a new life somewhere away from the influence of family and friends.

"We would be unequally yoked," he told her. "With each passing day, a fire burns in my soul to tell people about Yeshua. I will never regret my decision."

Benjamin left soon after for seminary school.

Sarai never married. She was engaged once, years ago to a Jewish surgeon who worked at the Mount Sinai Hospital of Queens.

The trip to New York following his father's death had been short, and Sarai was still engaged at the time. They had spoken only briefly and in a polite, cursory manner.

Sarai worked for an insurance company that was having an annual meeting in San Francisco one year. Benjamin would be there the same week. Yes, she would have time for dinner, and yes, she would accompany him to a special Jews for Jesus presentation on Haight Street.

Benjamin was elated. Perhaps this was the Lord's timing, he thought.

The teacher painstakingly, with great detail and exactness, paralleled Old Testament Scriptures with New Testament passages of Jesus's birth and earthly ministry. How can she not be convinced? Benjamin thought.

Afterward they went for coffee. Neither spoke for the longest time. Finally, Sarai looked intently at Benjamin. It was the same deep, melancholy gaze he had seen so many years before.

"I'm sorry. Not a day goes by that I don't think of you and what our lives could have been together. For our sake, I wish I could believe. I'm so sorry, Benjamin, but I can't."

They parted, and in leaving, she gave him a present—a necklace with a gold cross enshrouded in the Star of David.

The road wound through fields of ponderosa pines and meadows bordered by split-rail log fences. Benjamin circled the lake, catching glimpses between the pines of the glittering water sparkling between the breaks in the ice.

His thoughts shifted from Sarai to Faith Gospel Tabernacle to the weekly prayer group. He reflected on the men's transparency during their recent time of confession and knew that they were making progress.

As he descended the mountain, his mind was racing

with details about the prayer assembly: evening format, Scripture passages to pray about, worship songs to sing.

As Benjamin reflected on the prayer assembly, he lifted his arms in victory. He kept both hands held high as he sprinted the final fifty yards to his car.

All of the men sensed that God was doing something in the city, even before Benjamin began organizing the group. When the clarion call came, each man obeyed the still, small voice of the Holy Spirit and agreed to meet weekly to pray for God's move in their land.

Chapter Six

It was snowing heavily when Benjamin left the church and began the drive home that Wednesday night. There were several inches on the ground, and the storm didn't appear to be letting up. Benjamin drove by the motels and then the jewelry stores before leaving the commercial district and driving into the five-mile checkerboard of county, state, and reservation lands. The snow hurtled against the windshield, providing small beams of light in an otherwise black December night.

The car ahead of Benjamin swerved rapidly and moved to pass a slowly moving van ahead of it when suddenly the vehicle went into a spin and ended up in the empty lane for oncoming traffic. The car halted and then began driving slowly back in the direction it had come from. "Thank you, Lord," Benjamin said aloud.

The neon lights on the downtown jewelry storefronts flashed for an instant, one last time, as Benjamin drove through a small curved ravine, removing visibility and leaving the downtown completely hidden.

A car following Benjamin pulled into the left lane alongside Benjamin. The dome light was on, and the man in the passenger seat looked intently toward Benjamin. He was a middle-aged man—Arabic, Benjamin noticed. The car slowed and then settled back into the lane, dropping to a distance of five or six car lengths behind Benjamin.

A mile and several minutes passed, and Benjamin turned right and began ascending a hill leading to the Monterey area. The car followed, its headlights reflecting in the rearview mirror. Benjamin noticed that the car was getting closer—perhaps fifteen to twenty yards back. A few minutes later Benjamin turned left. Again, the car followed.

Benjamin felt apprehensive. The pattern of turns was not extraordinary, necessarily, but he had a strange sense that he was being followed by the car with the Arabic man in the passenger seat.

He turned right on Cibola Boulevard. The headlights in his rearview mirror vanished momentarily, but then emerged as the car continued behind Benjamin.

If they turn again, I will know, Benjamin thought. At that moment, Benjamin and the Arab man were in the only two cars heading east in a snowstorm that was providing increasingly less visibility. There was no visible oncoming traffic. The open space in the fields leading to Monterey was black, with only the snow and the occasional streetlight altering the color of the darkened night. As they approached Red Bluff Estates, Benjamin accelerated and turned right rapidly, spinning slightly but quickly straightening out his GMC SUV. The vehicle was heavy and performed well on ice. He drove one block and swerved right again and then stopped—no lights behind. The car was gone. Benjamin dropped his head and closed his eyes. He jerked at the tap on his window and saw the police beacon light from the rearview mirror. Had he fallen asleep? He rolled the window down and squinted as large flakes pelted his face. There were two officers, several yards apart.

"Can I see your driver's license, please?"

Benjamin handed the officer his driver's license.

"Where are you going, Mr. Sharon?"

"I'm heading home from the church I pastor. Is there a problem?"

"You were driving very erratically. Are you okay?"

"Did you see the car following . . .?" Benjamin stopped himself. "I'm sorry. I'll be home in a few minutes. I'll be careful, officer."

"Have a good night, Pastor Sharon. Yes, please do be careful."

Benjamin turned the vehicle around, left the estates, and proceeded to drive home. Where was the car? How did it disappear as quickly as it came? Why didn't the police officers see it?

The following week at the men's prayer meeting, Benjamin announced the prayer assembly:

"Yeshua has placed something of great importance upon my heart that I must share with you. The church is filled with cold hearts—even worse, lukewarm hearts.

People that have heard the gospel message time and again and are no longer moved—a comfortable church masquerading under the term 'blessing.' As watchmen on the walls, we must be heralds sounding the call to prayer. We must bridge the gap for our city and provide opportunity for the people to walk over the chasm of sin by clinging to Yeshua. We must provide a forum for believers to come to, and we must pray that God softens hearts.

"I have been called by Yeshua to pastor Faith Gospel Tabernacle. It is a great privilege, and I labor earnestly in that calling. I have developed a great love for the Navajo people and the Hispanic people too. But I have also been called to unite the Christians in this area to seek a great move of God among us. I will be obedient to that call.

"My ministry is not ecumenical. My belief system does not embrace an interfaith theology. Yeshua, Jesus, said, 'I am the way, the truth, and the life: no man cometh unto the Father, but by me.' There is only one way to heaven—not multiple ways.

"In Ephesians, Paul references a point of maturity in our faith when he says, under the power of the Holy Spirit, 'until finally we all believe alike about our salvation and about our Savior, God's Son, and all become full-grown in the Lord—yes, to the point of being filled full with Christ' (Ephesians 4:13 TLB).

"We know that there are certain truths that cannot be negotiated. We understand this well.

"But there are doctrinal issues that are difficult. There are distinctives among us and among the body of Christ at large that should not separate us. These are issues that have divided great men and women of the faith in years past and continue to impact the church today. Oftentimes these differences are used by the enemy to divide us and hinder our effectiveness. The differences create factions within the church. Denominations and ultimately small enclave groups of believers emerge, each holding to what they think is the truth and, in many instances, distancing themselves from true brothers and sisters in Christ who do not share a particular creed.

"We must guard against this. The Lord is not pleased to see this disunity among us."

Benjamin paused and then recited the Nicene Creed.

"I believe in one God, the Father Almighty,
Maker of heaven and earth,
and of all things visible and invisible.

"And in one Lord Jesus Christ,
the only begotten Son of God,
begotten of the Father before all worlds;
God of God, Light of Light,
very God of very God; begotten, not made,
being of one substance with the Father,
by Whom all things were made.
Who, for us men for our salvation,
came down from heaven,
and was incarnate by the Holy Spirit of the
Virgin Mary,

and was made man;
and was crucified also for us under
Pontius Pilate;

"He suffered and was buried;
and the third day He rose again,
according to the Scriptures;
and ascended into heaven,
and sits on the right hand of the Father;
and He shall come again, with glory,
to judge the quick and the dead;
whose kingdom shall have no end.

"And I believe in the Holy Ghost,
the Lord and Giver of Life;
who proceeds from the Father and the Son;
who with the Father and the Son together is
worshipped and glorified;
who spoke by the prophets.

"And I believe in one holy catholic and
apostolic Church.
I acknowledge one baptism for the remission
of sins;
and I look for the resurrection of the dead,
and the life of the world to come.

Amen."

Benjamin paused and looked at the men. "We may not agree on all doctrinal matters, but I think it's safe to say that we agree on these central tenets of the faith. Amen?"

The men followed with a resounding "Amen!"

Benjamin continued. "We agree that doctrine is important. We're all to grow in the grace and knowledge of Jesus Christ and remain not babes in Christ but become mature people of the faith, understanding our heritage in Yeshua and learning more and more of the depth of His glorious Word. But, where possible, we should not exclude our Christian brothers. Love must override some of our differences.

"We will invite Christian leaders from the area—not just our own group. However, I understand that there are those who are so locked in tradition that they'll never join.

"We will glorify Yeshua in our prayers and pray about critical issues that face our city. The Scripture range will be broad, Full Gospel.

"I'm not looking for a response today. But I ask each of you to pray earnestly and ask the Lord if He is in this. We will talk again next week."

There was great exuberance in the prayers that followed, and whatever concerns may have been felt among the men were hidden beneath the enthusiasm of coming together to petition God for a great move in the city.

That afternoon Benjamin sat in his study meditating on Scripture and thoughtfully planning the following year's sermon series. He loved *The Living Bible* for its eloquence but committed Scripture to memory from the Holy Bible King James Version. This next year he would preach chronologically from the Bible, beginning in Genesis with a message titled "In the Beginning." He would use *The Reese Chronological Bible* to determine the historical time frames, and would use the *Zondervan Handbook to the Bible* and the Hebrew Bible as study guides. The pictorial aids in Zondervan's were rich in Jewish history. Benjamin would include stone jars, pottery, a prayer shawl, and a shofar, as well as other Jewish artifacts as visuals. The sermons would provide a historical setting with application for the believer in Christ today. Interspersed in the Old Testament chronological series would be special messages. In December, during Jewish Hanukkah, Benjamin would teach on the Maccabees. There would be instructional segments on the Old Testament feasts. A dramatic film presentation of the Holy Land, presenting historical biblical settings including a segment on the Valley of Megiddo, would be shown to the congregation with special emphasis on inviting the community at large. There would be adult Sunday school classes—a class on the Hebrew language, a prophetic class titled "Prophesies About the Messiah," and an evangelism class for young adults called "The Young Warriors." He would teach a special series titled *Simchat Torah–Rejoicing With the Torah.*

Benjamin cherished the Old Testament and marveled at the providential symmetry between the old and new covenants. Each plan, perfectly conceived in eternity past, each plan perfectly implemented in Jehovah's timing.

Chapter Seven

While Benjamin was working on his sermon series, Alexander Joseph was completing the outline for the class he would be teaching that semester at the college—Religious Studies: Great Historical Christian Revivals. For the last term, he taught on prominent biblical revivals, with emphasis on Nineveh and on Acts 2. This class would learn of the First Great Awakening.

He would also be showing The Sentinel Group's *Transformations* series—documentaries of extraordinary moves of God throughout the world.

The class was mixed culturally, ethnically, and religiously. Sixty-five percent of the students were Navajo, matching the demographics of the area closely, with some of the students holding to traditional Navajo beliefs. Twenty percent were Hispanic, primarily Catholic. The remaining students were Anglo, other than one Muslim student.

The gospel would be presented clearly and forcefully within the curriculum, and Alexander would frequently say, "I am available to meet with any of you away from class, at which time I will be privileged to answer other questions you may have."

He had led four students in salvation prayers the prior semester.

The men managed to avoid tension over church doctrine, primarily because they didn't discuss doctrinal distinctions and denominational differences. Opinions were expressed lightly and gently; they refrained from open debates and were sensitive to avoid inflammatory remarks. They came together and laughed, shared about their week's work, and, without specifically mentioning names, touched on the struggles they endured in their congregations. They teased each other, laughed at themselves occasionally, and prayed.

Individually, each man held tenaciously to the inerrancy of the Word of God, the deity of Christ, the triune God, the eternal nature of man's soul, and the fact that salvation was granted by grace through faith. They shunned a works salvation and embraced the reformation. Beyond those tenets, they held profound differences that were not unchallenged as they came together to seek the Lord's face.

David Janssen was a reluctant member of the group, given the historical apprehension on the part of the Wisconsin Synod's leadership to mix with other Protestant denominations.

He divided the modern-day church of America into three categories: First, there were the Mennonites, Amish,

Quakers, Holiness Methodists, and every other group that was willing to separate themselves from the world and all it represented. This meant television, movies, and any number of other activities "soiled" by the world. He believed that the passage referencing a "peculiar people" was truly describing a separate people, a people whose lives were distanced from the things of this world.

"Yes, there are differences within the denominations," Benjamin would challenge. "But which group is right? They all have doctrinal differences."

But it wasn't simply the doctrinal creeds that tied them together, David thought, but rather, their willingness to separate from a world gone awry.

Then secondly, there were the Pentecostals and all of the associated movements. This included the prophetic movement, the word of knowledge movement, the word of faith movement, and the prosperity movement—movements that David felt had failed to embrace a balanced scriptural view.

And finally, there were the countless numbers of seeker-friendly churches—large or small—that failed to preach repentance for fear of alienating a church body that was bent more on motivational and feel-good messages than on serving a risen Savior that demanded holiness from a redeemed people.

Compton Atherton never preached categorically for Arminianism or against Calvinism, but when questioned by a parishioner in private counseling sessions, he would say, "I'm a zero-point Calvinist." He would then delineate the TULIP—the acronymic term describing the five tenets of Calvinism—by rebutting each, one by one:

"T" is for Total Depravity, meaning that man is utterly evil with no capability of his own to obtain righteousness. Compton agreed with that premise, but he felt it a moot point to argue that, inherently, man possessed nothing apart from God. It was impossible, Compton would say, to separate His creation completely from His design. Just by nature of being created by God provided for a measure of good. Man is born into sin, but with a God-given capacity for good.

He would detail the Arminian position against Unconditional Election, Limited Atonement, Irresistible Grace, and then culminate his presentation by saying, "And yes, a believer can walk away from the faith. This is warned against throughout the Epistles."

Compton loved the great hymns of the faith and appreciated contemporary praise music. He had grown up with Southern Gospel. His ultimate music experience would to be one of the "friends" in a Gaither setting.

Though he shunned the term "hyper-Calvinist," doctrinally, Robert Thompson was a dyed-in-the-wool Calvinist. He quoted Whitefield and ignored Wesley. He read from Luther and Spurgeon but gave little time to Moody. He taught a class on Edwards' "Sinners in the Hands of an Angry God" but denied a request to teach on Finney's *The Key to Revival*. Robert loved Sproul, MacArthur, and Kennedy, criticized Hunt, and only tolerated Wilkerson and Hayford. In a twist of irony, he admired Billy Graham. "Graham," Robert would say, "is above the debate."

One of Nathanial Allan's most oft quoted passages was "Jesus Christ is the same yesterday, today, and forever" (Hebrews 13:8 NKJV). The gifts were for today just as they were two thousand years ago. The reason we didn't see miracles today is because of unbelief. Even Jesus, in His hometown of Nazareth "did not many mighty works there because of their unbelief" (Matthew 13:58). Nathanial had seen miracles. He had seen miraculous healings that medical doctors could not explain.

Nathanial had thick, wavy brown hair and wore a thigh-length black leather jacket that had worn away at the right elbow, leaving a hollowed space in the otherwise smooth garment. "A battle scar," Nathanial would say. "But not like the battle scars on my knees," he would add.

Nathanial was a prayer warrior, oftentimes spending an hour or more in prayer, on many days arising before dawn to seek the Lord for direction.

Nathanial appreciated Benjamin's zeal and passion for prayer and the lost. He appreciated Alexander's instructive teaching on revival. He would lift those men up before the Lord frequently. He would also lift up the needs of the pastors of every other life-breathing, gospel-preaching church in the area.

He would support Benjamin's plan. Nathanial, too, was certain that Mountain Fire would see revival.

As much as possible, Gary Smith stayed clear of doctrinal discussions. God loved the world so much that

He sent Jesus to die for the sins of everyone who would put their faith in Him. The grace to believe was freely available to all. That's what he knew. That's what he preached.

Jack Broholm considered himself a connoisseur of great preaching. He could travel the country for a year and hear a different preacher every week. He had heard each man preach and loved each one of them. Each particular style contained its own subtleties, some with flair, others very much polished and refined.

He especially appreciated Benjamin's style of building to a crescendo. Under the unction of the Holy Spirit, Benjamin would close a thought with a rapid succession of phrasing that typically culminated in five hundred or, had it been a larger church, one thousand or three thousand amens. No one did the crescendos like Benjamin; not Compton Atherton, not Nathanial Allan or any other Pentecostal preacher that Jack had ever heard—not even J. Franklin, although he was close.

After Benjamin, Robert Thompson was Jack's favorite. "The key in a fluent message," Robert would tell him, "is the transitional phrasing." He would then quickly qualify: "I agree with Alexander. The most important ingredient in any message is the anointing of the Holy Spirit. Scripted, memorized, or extemporaneous, the leading of the Holy Spirit has to be there. Without His anointing, you might as well go home."

Jack cherished his relationship with the men. He appreciated the diversity in their preaching styles.

Jacob Randall believed in election but also believed in the Great Commission. He was not dogmatic on any number of doctrines and, in keeping with EFCA, was tolerant, if not accepting, of other mainline Protestant denominations.

His personal doctrinal views were very much Protestant but somewhat eclectic. In respect to the return of the Lord, he had vacillated between a pretribulation, midtribulation, and posttribulation position over the course of his Christian walk, finally settling on prewrath: the Christian would endure some suffering during the great tribulation but would be spared the ultimate, climactic horror of the final wrath of God before the second coming of Jesus.

He accepted that the sign gifts were present today even though many in his denomination felt otherwise and even though he himself did not speak in tongues. The end of these special gifts, as referenced in 1 Corinthians 13:8, and that the present-day sign gift detractors often quoted, would clearly come in a new age. Clearly this verse was speaking of a future church age after the Lord's return. What a stretch, Jacob thought, to suggest that the church had entered a new age just after the disciples died.

Justin Randall's exposure to revival was twofold. One, after reading David Yonggi Cho's book *Prayer That Brings Revival*, he had visited Prayer Mountain in Seoul, South Korea, with an interdenominational group of believers. To see believers laying prostrate in prayer, in small enclaves, for hours on end, had moved him to a greater life of solitary prayer. Justin's prayer life was still not where he felt that it should be, but he had set aside a time each week to pray for the men, to lift up their families, and pray for the needs of their congregations.

And he visited the Brownsville Assembly of God, from which he came back and said, "It's true. God is moving powerfully in Pensacola."

Justin had little time for dogmatism. His favorite verse from the Psalms was, "But You are holy, Enthroned in the praises of Israel" (Psalm 22:3 NKJV). "Lift your voices," he would say to the congregation. "God inhabits the praises of His people."

As close as their friendship was, Benjamin and Alexander disagreed on a number of doctrinal distinctives, though they generally kept discussion of those differences to a minimum.

Just days after Benjamin had shared his vision of the prayer assembly with Alexander, the men had accepted—and not without considerable reservations—an invitation to debate the subject "Freewill – Arminianism or Calvinism?" to a group of seminary students in Santa Fe.

Benjamin took the podium and began: "There are five offices of the Holy Spirit—pastor, teacher, evangelist, apostle, and prophet. Theologian is not one of them. I'm not saying they can't be saved." Alexander chuckled; the students laughed lightly.

"My theology is not defined by the name of a mere man. It's defined by the eternal, triune God of the

Bible—Elohim, Yeshua, Jesus the Christ, the Messiah to all who will believe, to all who will trust Him with their lives. There is a simplicity in the gospel message that has been discarded by the theologians and those who spend so much of their lives trying to define God. The Bible says, 'For God so loved the world, that he gave his only begotten Son, that whosoever believeth in him should not perish, but have everlasting life.' Yeshua said, 'Come unto me, all ye that labour and are heavy laden, and I will give you rest.' And, 'Whosoever will, let him take the water of life freely.' Do you believe that these Scripture verses are just rhetorical in nature? I believe that these passages point to God's invitation to all of humanity to come and enter into a relationship with His Son, Jesus. I believe that the grace to believe is available to all. My friend here will state that God imparts the grace to believe selectively—that only some have the opportunity to be saved. You are a learned man of God," Benjamin said, turning to Alexander, "but we differ in our interpretation of what God is saying to mankind.

"Prayer, evangelism, and reading the Word are not mere exercises in the faith. They are, in the analogy of warfare, of combat, weapons that God uses to bring about victory in the life of a believer in Christ and in the lives of those that are perishing outside the cross.

"Some theologians today confine our faith to spiritual microchips. I believe that position has misrepresented Scripture. God is sovereign—His power is infinite—but He has given man a free will to choose or reject Him."

Alexander took the podium and expounded on the orthodox view of Calvinism. He referenced the leading proponents throughout church history of the doctrine of election, while also mentioning men of faith that believed in foreknowledge. "None of us disagree on that point," he said. "We all understand that God is omnipotent—He's all-powerful. He's omnipresent—He's everywhere. And He's omniscient—He knows about everything: everything in eternity past, everything in eternity future. And that includes who will be saved."

Alexander felt uncomfortable. With other men of God, relationships might have been strained leading to division and separation. He and Benjamin had avoided this stress, each maintaining respect in the midst of a difficult doctrine. Alexander believed that God was doing something extraordinary in Mountain Fire. He also recognized a dichotomy with his brand of Calvinism. Did accepting the five points of Calvinism in their entirety mean accepting what some theologians had titled "double predestination," with some holding to the belief that God had predestined the elect to eternal life in heaven while also predestining the rest of mankind to eternal damnation in hell? Even now, at seventy-one years of age, Alexander had been unable to reconcile that position. Would God, in His supreme love, invite man into a relationship with Himself, knowing that man in himself had no ability to believe? The reformer would teach that man's will is always bent toward his own desires, that man would not nor could not of his own will choose God without the Holy Spirit first providing the very grace needed to even cry out to Him for salvation. And yet, how could unconditional election be reconciled with the Scripture passage from 2 Peter 3:9 stating, "The Lord is not slack concerning His promise, as some count slackness, but is longsuffering toward us, not willing that any should perish but that all should come to repentance" (NKJV)? And the Revelation passage, "And the Spirit and the bride say, Come. And let him that heareth say, Come. And let him that is athirst come. And whosoever will ['Whoever desires' NKJV], let him take the water of life freely" (Revelation 22:17).

Reformed theology taught that nothing happens outside of God's sovereign plan. Yet Jesus, in talking about divorce in Matthew 19:8 said, "Moses, because of the hardness of your hearts, permitted you to divorce your wives, but from the beginning it was not so" (NKJV). In Genesis 6:6 the Word of God states, "And the LORD was sorry that He had made man on the earth, and He was grieved in His heart" (NKJV). To Ezekiel the question came, " 'Do I have any pleasure at all that the wicked should die?' says the Lord GOD, 'and not that he should turn from his ways and live?' " (Ezekiel 18:23 NKJV); "Say to them: 'As I live,' says the Lord GOD, 'I have no pleasure in the death of the wicked, but that the wicked turn from his way and live. Turn, turn from your evil ways! For why should you die, O house of Israel?' " (Ezekiel 33:11 NKJV). The reformer would say that even sin was ordained by God, for His glory. Yet James said, "Let no one say when he is tempted, 'I am tempted by God'; for God cannot be tempted by evil, nor does He Himself tempt anyone. But each one is tempted when he is drawn away by his own desires and enticed" (James 1:13-14 NKJV).

Alexander was distraught. The profundity of election was beyond his understanding. During these moments of questioning, he agonized over the depths and gravity of both Calvinism and Arminianism. The turmoil he felt was overwhelming. How was he to comprehend such profound doctrines involving a sovereign and all-powerful God? *My Lord and my King! Who can comprehend the depth of Your wisdom?* he cried out in his spirit. Alexander knew from Jeremiah 17:9 that "The heart is deceitful above all things, and desperately wicked: who can know it?" Who was he to question God's election? God's judgments were true, His precepts perfectly just. The apostle Paul had written in Romans 11, "Oh, the depth of the riches both of the wisdom and knowledge of God! How unsearchable are His judgments and His ways past finding out!" (Romans 11:33 NKJV). *Forgive me, Lord,* Alexander thought. *I know that You are a gracious, merciful, and righteous God. Your plan of salvation was founded in perfect wisdom. My love for You will never change. Please help me to understand.*

Benjamin believed that an apostate church existed today. But the true church of Jesus Christ, comprised of many tongues and nations and creeds—and doctrinal differences on some points—was not in danger of ecumenicalism. Rather, the threat the church had been succumbing to for over a half a century was apathy.

Alexander believed that the truly elect could not walk away from their salvation. Benjamin believed in abiding faith.

Benjamin was there at Alexander's request. He didn't enjoy the debate. He believed that it was a subject best left in academia for professors and theologians—some of whom had missed the most important lesson in life: they didn't know Yeshua.

Yet, just as Alexander had doubts on election, Benjamin, too, had struggled with his view of man's free will. He wrestled with the Arminian interpretation of Romans 8 and 9. How was the passage involving "vessels of destruction" not clear? Throughout the Bible, God's providence and divine governance were clearly manifest in the affairs of man. With exactness and precision, the parameters of history had been set in place. Events in the book of Revelation were immutable. Boundaries and measurements were established by God's decree, His edicts unchangeable. Days and weeks and months and time had been established with no variance possible. Proverbs 16:9 says, "A man's heart plans his way, But the LORD directs his steps" (NKJV). Were the actions and destiny of each man's life also predetermined?

In the midst of these doubts, Benjamin held to the Scripture passage from John 3:17: "For God sent not his Son into the world to condemn the world; but that the world through him might be saved."

Paul, under the anointing of the Holy Spirit, wrote of an urgency in proclaiming the gospel message, an imperative which Benjamin embraced fervently: "Knowing therefore the terror of the LORD, we persuade men" (2 Corinthians 5:11). My calling, Benjamin thought, is to proclaim the gospel to all who will hear.

Chapter Eight

It was exactly eight o'clock, and the hall was packed when Benjamin approached the podium. After several opening comments, he got right to the point.

"It's ludicrous that Israel would release nine hundred prisoners. It's a travesty that the United States of America would support and encourage such a gesture. It's unforgivable and unthinkable that the president and secretary of state would present this as part of a peace initiative. This would be like the administration releasing nine hundred political prisoners in the United States who had pledged to assassinate the president.

"Israel should hold to the established territories. She should not have given up Bethlehem; she should not have given up Jericho; she should hold onto Gaza and not relinquish the West Bank. Ever!"

"Occupied territories," a man yelled out.

"The West Bank is necessary for Israel's security," Benjamin responded.

A large part of the crowd erupted in cheers, but the

hissing and screams of "fraud" were not unnoticed by Benjamin as he continued.

The rage that was interspersed throughout the crowd had not been expected. Benjamin had gone to the town hall meeting in Flagstaff with the intent of lending support to a local conservative Christian, pro-Israeli initiative, with no thought whatsoever of seeing Abdul, let alone enduring the public humiliation he felt when Abdul screamed out, "You're a phony," just as the meeting ended.

The next morning, Benjamin sat down in Alexander's office and handed him a letter.

Pastor Benjamin Sharon
Faith Gospel Tabernacle
777 Juniper Lane
Mountain Fire, NM 87817

The President
The White House
1600 Pennsylvania Avenue, N.W.
Washington, D.C. 20500

Dear Mr. President:

I know you are extremely busy, but I would ask you respectfully to please read this letter in its entirety and then pray about what I have written. Please do not be offended. Accept these "hard words" as what I believe to be a message from the Lord.

My primary purpose in this letter is to encourage you in your faith to uncompromisingly, regardless of the political consequences, elevate Yeshua, Jesus Christ, as the only answer to the ultimate fate of this nation. If you fail to do so, I believe that your legacy for all of eternity will be altered.

As you know, the country is diametrically opposed—politically, philosophically, and spiritually. You were elected, providentially, even though you did not, in reality, garner a majority vote. You were elected because, in many ways, you have been willing to stand up against evil. May we rejoice together and praise the God of the Bible for that courage!

The Bible says, "Trust in the LORD with all your heart, And lean not on your own understanding; In all your ways acknowledge Him, And He shall direct your paths" (Proverbs 3:5-6 NKJV).

Mindful of that Scripture passage, this is no time in history to be pandering to false religions or political groups that do not represent the truth. Rather, be direct; be bold. Jesus said, "I am the way, the truth, and the life: no man cometh unto the Father, but by me." You either believe that or you don't. If you do, proclaim it unabashedly and let God take care of the rest. Your primary life's work is not to be president of the United States, but rather to obey Jesus Christ regardless of the cost.

Many of the problems that we face as a country are monumental and may only be solved in a limited manner. Concentrate your focus on a limited agenda that has lasting, eternal consequences. Make your commitment to Jesus—that you will battle abortion, support Israel unflinchingly, support true marriage between man and woman, fight evil, tell the truth unabashedly, and then, let Yeshua, Jesus, be your rock and defender. Without Him fighting your battle, your agenda is of little consequence.

In response to the question, "Where do I draw the line?" the answer is, you go all the way, one hundred percent. Whatever He tells you to do, you do—regardless of the consequences. Let your legacy be that you were obedient in every way, that you did what was right in the sight of the Lord.

We must all count the cost. We must all stand up and be counted for truth. That applies to the highest office in the land and to the lowest servant as well.

I send this to you humbly; I know how weak I am at certain moments in life. You are in an incredibly difficult position, and the pressure has to be overwhelming at times. I ask you to take everything that I've written in the respectful manner in which it is intended.

Thank you for taking the time to read this letter. May Yeshua bless you with the courage to obey Him, whatever the cost. Please let me know if you would like to talk further.

Most respectfully,

Pastor Benjamin Sharon

Alexander read the letter thoughtfully. "Did you send it?"

"Yes. Last night."

"No one will ever accuse you of lacking chutzpah." Alexander smiled.

"In fairness, I did hesitate. You know, Alex, that Yeshua is the consuming fire in my life. He's called me to a life and ministry of prayer and evangelism, and of shepherding a flock with needs that are indescribable. I will never disregard His call. The political arena will always be a distant second in regard to my calling. But it occurs to me that we can't simply implore Yeshua to change our city without being willing vessels for good in His hands. We can't pray for God to revive our land and stand idly by while evil has free rein. Yeshua cannot be pleased by the apathy He sees today in our country."

Benjamin paused and looked at his friend.

"Alex, I am particularly troubled by the release of prisoners in Gaza. I'm distraught when I think of such lunacy."

"The Lord is in control. The Middle East will not rest, other than momentarily, until the Lord returns. I will pray that you stay focused on the work that God has put before you."

"Yeshua knows I am eternally grateful for your prayers. Shalom, my friend."

Benjamin turned and left.

The following Thursday, the men convened for their weekly prayer meeting. As they sat in their customarily circular fashion, Benjamin scanned their faces for an indication of their response.

Jack Broholm spoke first. "Count me in. I'll help get the word out. I'll contact the newspaper and radio stations."

"This is not a marketing event," Robert Thompson objected.

"No, it's not," Benjamin responded. "But Yeshua does expect us to make a public pronouncement. We are calling the people to come and assemble at His feet. We have to inform the community. In doing so, Yeshua will bless the work of our hands, but it will be Him who quickens the hearts and brings the people to the assembly. The call is to God's people, but if a nonbeliever comes and receives Yeshua's grace, then to Yeshua be the glory."

"What about tongues?" David Janssen asked. "Yeshua is a God of order. The Word of God says if there are tongues in a public service, there should be an interpreter. We must be obedient to the Word of God. With that in mind, we must guard against being so rigid that the Holy Spirit is quenched. We will not inhibit forms of worship that are in the Bible."

"Will we invite Catholics?" Jacob Randall asked. "There are Catholics that know Yeshua as Savior and, just as in our churches, others that do not. Let's pray that anyone trusting in Mary for salvation will be introduced to Yeshua, Jesus, the only One who can save a man's soul. Let's pray that if someone is trusting in good works or church membership, that Yeshua's death on Calvary will be made clear."

Robert Thompson committed to praying earnestly for the assembly but hesitated on making an aggressive effort in asking his congregation to attend.

Benjamin responded softly but firmly. "Your congregation must come. If you fail to invite them, you're not really with us. At least those that attend your weekly prayer meeting should be there. But that is not enough. We need to urge every member of our flocks to come. This is of grave and urgent importance."

"You know I'm in, Benjamin," Gary Smith said. "I will give a poster to Emily for the bookstore."

"My congregation will be there," Nathanial declared as he leapt to his feet and pumped his fist. "Yes! Hallelujah!"

"I have written a letter that will be sent to two hundred churches within a ninety-mile radius of Mountain Fire. We will invite the pastors and congregations to come and seek God's face for revival in our land."

Benjamin read a portion of the letter. "As Christians, we believe that we are one body—not multiple bodies. We believe that denominational barriers have been erected by man—not by God. We urge you, knowing that the season is at hand and the time is short, to join us on the twentieth of January two thousand and six for an evening of praise and worship to our King."

Benjamin looked up from the letter. "The auditorium seats twelve hundred. We will come together and cry out to Yeshua for healing in our land. Like Nehemiah, we will rebuild the walls and hang the gates of our city. We will do it through prayer."

One by one the men spoke. Compton Atherton agreed to aggressively promote the assembly to his congregation. Jacob Randall expressed the desire to help in whatever way he could.

Each of the men agreed to pray aloud at the assembly; various Scripture passages would be prayerfully considered and decided upon in the coming days.

Benjamin looked at Justin Randall. "And you, my friend, will lead the worship under the Lord." Justin nodded, smiled, and looked to the ceiling, lifting his right hand skyward. He closed his eyes and began singing softly:

"When I survey the wondrous cross
On which the Prince of glory died,
My richest gain I count but loss,
And pour contempt on all my pride."

Justin stood and reached for the hand of Compton Atherton on his one side and Jacob on the other side and lifted their hands to heaven. The men stood in a circle, hands lifted, and began singing along with Justin.

The singing continued for several minutes, and then the men began praying, individually, aloud, each proclaiming God's majesty and glory. Finally, the din subsided, and the group stood silently, whispering over and over, "Jesus, Jesus, Jesus."

Alexander spoke last. "All of you know where I stand. For most of my life this is what I've been praying for. If God called us to put on sackcloth and sit in ashes, I would be there. I'll pray that the body of Christ responds to the call to assemble for prayer. I'll encourage my students, even though most of them are not saved, to attend the assembly and experience God's grace. God will be with us, I know. Truly, He is holy."

Chapter Nine

There comes a time in every man's life when he must choose whom he will serve. For some, the decision comes just after the age of reason and has consequences that last for a lifetime. For others, the decision is postponed month to month, year to year, until the last dying breath in this world removes the hope of eternal life for all who will believe.

For the Christian, too, comes a moment of truth: Jesus said, "If you love Me, you will keep My commandments" (John 14:15 NASB).

No sooner had Benjamin obeyed the Lord and called the prayer assembly, than the enemy came in like a flood. For weeks, he had been speaking on the phone with a woman named Natasha. She was the managing partner of a Christian supply house and art gallery in Albuquerque. Benjamin had been talking to her about decorative art for Faith Gospel Tabernacle.

The conversations were at first infrequent—once every other week, then once a week, then daily, and finally, after speaking for several weeks, twice a day.

Benjamin was surprised when he saw her. She was tall—five feet nine, perhaps five feet ten, Benjamin thought. She had deep burgundy hair that fell beyond her shoulders. Their eyes met and she smiled. It was the most captivating smile Benjamin had ever seen.

"Good morning, Pastor Sharon. I'm so happy we can finally meet." She extended her hand. It was soft and her eyes sparkled as Benjamin extended his hand and momentarily held hers.

"Hello, Natasha. Yes, at long last." Benjamin silently rebuked the attraction he felt as the two walked through the gallery reviewing the artwork.

An hour later, Benjamin was leaving Albuquerque, unable, or so he thought, to think of anything but his encounter with Natasha. He was troubled. He couldn't believe that with everything else happening in his life that he would suddenly be attracted to a woman whom he just recently had met, knew nothing about, and hardly knew. He prayed, "God, help me. Remove these feelings. I don't even know her. Why am I feeling this way?"

That night, Benjamin had a dream. He was running along the familiar path he often ran on. It was dusk, and bolts of lightning flashed before him, creating an asymmetrical tapestry throughout the sky. Benjamin felt a pain in his chest—his heart. He felt a heaviness as he ran and watched in fear as the lightning shot to the ground in front of him. Benjamin knew he was in danger and turned back. And then he awakened.

Benjamin knew the meaning of the dream. The Lord impressed that upon him the moment he awakened. He had been hurt, injured (the pain over his heart), and in his injured state he had persisted in moving in a direction that the Lord had warned him against. He was literally running into a storm that threatened his life before he sensed the Holy Spirit urging him to turn and go back.

He went to his study and began reading from the Psalms. He then spent an hour in prayer before the Lord. He confessed a distracted heart, carried away like the wind in a moment of sensuality and fantasy. He confessed a host of other sins—pride, ego, fear, unbelief, and failing to be diligent in the cause that Yeshua had put before him.

As he reflected on his thoughts about Natasha, Benjamin remembered one of the confessions from an earlier prayer meeting. "Sometimes, it seems, we're but a suggestion away from sin's grasp. A smile, a whisper from the evil one and we would all fall prey—but by the grace and power of Jesus."

Benjamin felt as if he had lost two months of his life. And to some extent he had.

Suddenly, he was overcome with anger and cried out with a loud voice, "Get behind me, Satan! Demons of darkness—flee from me in the mighty name of Yeshua!"

As he began his run that evening, the sunset unveiled a kaleidoscope sky—a prism of orange and yellows, blues and reds, a tapestry of gold and pastel colors that sparkled in the evening sky. Benjamin breathed deeply and whispered aloud. "Yeshua, Adonai. Praise You, dear God. You are truly awesome!"

The cloud had lifted. He never thought of her in that way again.

"Listen carefully, students.

"There are two primary characteristics, and I believe two necessary ingredients, that are seen in virtually all of the great Christian revivals I've studied.

"And those prerequisites, if you will, are number one, a deep and thorough repentance of sin among God's people, and secondly, a desperate, fervent crying out to God for His presence in their midst.

"Let's examine these criteria for revival. The people of Nineveh, for example, from the king on down to the servants, in recognition of their impending doom, literally put on sackcloth—a coarse garment of the day that was worn during periods of mourning—and sat in the streets and covered their heads with ashes. This was done to display true repentance and humility toward the One who controlled their destinies. This humiliation was to display publicly a willingness to turn away from their sin and evil practices. Throughout historical revivals, we see this time and time again. The people confess their sins to Almighty God, with a willingness to forsake their evil, and then God, in turn, restores their land.

"Their transgressions may be sins of commission—in other words, blatant sinful actions against God's commands, sinful deeds that the people are guilty of. Or, they may be sins of omission—failure to carry out the directives that God has given them, which constitutes a failure to fully surrender their lives to the lordship of the one true God.

"And then, having come to that place of complete surrender, and recognizing their utter dependence upon God for redemption, the people begin crying out to God. Not because God has difficulty hearing. God is not only omnipresent, which means that He's everywhere; He's not only omnipotent, which means that He's all-powerful. But He's omniscient—He knows everything: everything in eternity past, everything that is happening today, and everything that will happen in the future. He's not dependent on our voices to hear our cries from within. He knows our innermost thoughts. He knows our hearts. Rather, the cries are reflective of the sincere and deep anguish we sense when we become aware of the sin and disobedience in our lives and we beseech God to touch and heal our cold hearts."

Alexander paused from his lecture and took a drink from a glass of water on his desk. "Preach it, my friend!" Benjamin had said the last time he sat in on one of Alexander's classes and heard the professor speak with such passion.

Alexander wished he were speaking to every Christian believer in the country, not merely twenty-two unsaved students in Mountain Fire, New Mexico—a place most people had never even heard of.

Alexander placed the glass on the oak desk, causing a deep rumble in the otherwise silent classroom. Every eye was on him, and it occurred to him that he had rarely commanded this level of attention. The Lord is moving right now, he thought. It was important that he facilitate the Lord's work and not get in the way of the Holy Spirit.

" 'Today is the day of salvation,' the Bible says. 'When you hear His voice, harden not your hearts.'

"The class is adjourned. I will be going immediately to my car. If anyone has questions on today's lecture, I will be happy to meet with you in the parking lot and answer those concerns."

Chapter Ten

The car sped erratically through the narrow cobble-stone alley until it reached the end of the housing district, where it came to a sudden stop. Benjamin had replayed the scene in his mind a thousand times before. The men got out of the car and ran to the entryway of the three-story apartment building directly in front of the car. They entered the stairwell and began ascending the steps rapidly. Benjamin was out of breath after running a block from the crevice where he had been waiting. He entered the stairwell cautiously. He could hear the men at the top of the stairs. The stairwell was dark, but a light went on at the top. And then it was dark again, as the men closed the door behind them. This couldn't be, Benjamin thought. What if Micah was not on time? Did he even realize that Benjamin had left his post? The alleyway was almost black—the lights had been turned off hours before. Benjamin crept quietly past the door on the second-floor landing. He froze as he heard movement in the room. A faucet turned on and then off. What sounded like a glass hitting a counter resonated through the door, and then it was still again. As he climbed the cement steps he could hear muffled voices talking excitedly from behind the door at the top of the stairwell. Where was Micah? Where was his cover? Should he turn back and wait?

With no warning, the door opened like an explosion. Both men sprang from the room and headed for the steps. The light hit the landing like a beacon light in a prison yard. Benjamin slammed back against the cold wall and raised his gun. There was a look of horror on his face as the man in front saw Benjamin and screamed in Arabic. Benjamin understood the bloodcurdling cry that accompanied the "Kill the Jew" as the Palestinian raised his gun. Benjamin fired, and the man fell facedown toward him. The second man ran back into the room and slammed the door behind him, even as Benjamin raced down the stairs. Micah was waiting. The car had turned around in the narrow cul-de-sac, and Benjamin leaped into the passenger side.

Micah was screaming as he sped through the alley. "You were supposed to wait."

"You were supposed to be there," Benjamin yelled back.

In moments, they were at the end of the run. Micah parked the car perpendicular to the alley thoroughfare, clipped an explosive to the wiring under the dash, and the men ran to two awaiting cars. The cars left in opposite directions. As Benjamin rode off in the night he saw the burst of flames as the car in the alleyway exploded. The taillights of the car Micah was in became dimmer and dimmer until they were no longer in sight.

"What happened?" the driver asked. "Did you neutralize them?"

Benjamin closed his eyes and took a deep breath. He felt exhausted. "I got Khalid. Hafiz got away. They came at me suddenly, with no warning."

"They knew you were there?"

"No. They had no way of knowing. They were leaving for some reason. I don't know why."

"But he saw you? He knew it was you?"

"He knew. In the instant before he died. I don't think that Hafiz saw me."

The driver nodded thoughtfully and didn't say anything more as they drove off into the night.

Chapter Eleven

Alexander Joseph began his lecture by asking a series of questions: "Is it God's message, or is it your own message? How does a sermon become anointed by the Holy Spirit? Does a particular style of preaching contribute to the anointing?

"I meet weekly with a group of men to pray for revival. Each of them has a different style and method of preaching. Which is the most effective? Is there a style or method that is more God ordained than another?

"Listen closely. First and foremost, you must preach the message that God wants you to preach. Inherently, the anointing of the Holy Spirit will be upon you if you're obedient to delivering the message—no more, no less—that He places on your heart.

"Where the contemporary church errs is in trying to entertain. Fire-and-brimstone preachers of old would be run out of town by many modern-day congregations. Their church boards would fire the preacher, saying he was insensitive to the needs and diversity of the community. And yet, Jesus spoke more on hell than He did on heaven."

As Alexander was teaching on the anointing of the Holy Spirit, an underlying concern was nagging at him. There was a solemn mood at Thursday's prayer time that indicated something was wrong. The men weren't themselves. Talking was minimal. The typical lighthearted banter was missing. The prayers seemed mechanical. The usual cohesiveness in the group was absent.

The concern stayed with Alexander throughout Saturday and into the Sunday service. He couldn't completely put his hands around it, but a problem hung in the back of his mind like storm clouds darkening the sky. It involved the prayer assembly, he was certain. Little did he know how right he was.

As the prayer assembly got closer, the men began experiencing shock waves to their faith like tremors before an earthquake. Individually, each of the men knew that being covered in the blood, bathed in the Word, and shrouded in prayer were the divine insulators that would keep them immune from the tactics of the enemy and provide an impenetrable shield against the evil one. As time went on, the cracks in their armor became evident.

For David Janssen, the prior weeks had been uncharacteristically stressful. First, the prayer assembly announcement, which had been met by an uncanny silence from the congregation: no nodding, no apparent enthusiasm in their faces, no expression at all really—just stares.

And then, if the lack of response from the congregation wasn't enough, the call from Ron Stevens was unsettling.

"David, I want to say thank you! I enjoyed the service last Sunday very much!"

"Thank you, Ron."

"I appreciated your sermon. It was very eloquent, very compassionate. The congregation is blessed to have you as their pastor."

"I'm pleased that you were able to attend. Praise God that the message was meaningful to you!"

"I did want to ask you about the announcement I read in the bulletin about a prayer assembly. Is this an ecumenical gathering?"

"It's interdenominational, not interfaith."

"You realize that the church wouldn't approve, nonetheless?"

"I feel I have a responsibility to the city to participate."

"David, you have a responsibility to the synod to uphold the creeds and doctrines that separate us. You have a responsibility to the congregation to support and to maintain the church's position."

David was silent, unsure how to respond.

"The synod called you to minister in Mountain Fire, to maintain a presence for the liturgy entrusted to us. This is God's calling—for you and for me. David, I need to run. I know that you will do the right thing."

Jack Broholm was beside himself. He closed his eyes, tightened his lips together, and rubbed his eyelids with his thumb and forefinger before his hand slipped down across his face, stopping momentarily to slowly smooth out his mustache, matting the gray and black strands into two thin lines on his worried face. The grimace made way to a look of deep concern.

"I see. Thanks for letting me know."

His deal had just fallen through. In one fell swoop, a fifteen-thousand-dollar payday was out the window. On top of the incredible financial stress of the past three months, a $1.5 million resort acquisition project had just fallen through.

He laid the phone down and stared blankly at the file on his desk. The preliminary financial due diligence had been completed two months ago. He couldn't believe it. He should have known it was too good to be true. And yet, the bank was reputable. Even Equity One Source, Jack's primary lender, had spoken well of them. Given the small window of time that the loan needed to close in, Jack had agreed to give them the transaction.

Robinson, the loan originating officer, had said, "Bring us your deals. We're hungry. You'll find us very aggressive. We like motels and resorts, and we'll fund the loan faster than anyone else you're using."

That clinched it. Lending relationships were difficult to attract. Some of Jack's arrangements had taken years to cultivate. To have a lender initiate a call to him and then promise to fund the loan quickly was unheard of.

The project was a resort property in northern Minnesota. Ten cabins on five acres on a lake. Jack had been targeting resorts in Minnesota and Wisconsin and came across the project during a week of sales calls. In one week, over three hundred cold calls generated one loan project.

The deal was uncomplicated, almost boilerplate for Equity. A minority partner with good credit and a 40 percent stake in the business was buying out the majority owner. The sale price was $2 million, the borrower had 25 percent down, and the property appraisal came in at $2.2 million, which, after the down payment, gave the transaction a 68.2 percent loan-to-value ratio, well under the needed 80 percent. The debt-service coverage ratio was 1.5 to 1.8 the last three years. Jack seldom found deals this strong. But Equity couldn't fund the project as quickly as the borrower had required, so Jack pursued the loan with North Valley Bank, accepting a 1 percent commission instead of his customary 2 percent.

The bank issued the borrower a term sheet with an interest rate of Wall Street Journal Prime plus two. In the eleventh hour, the borrower said he needed 1.50 points over prime. The bank refused, and Jack's client took the loan to a local bank near the resort.

All they needed to do was match the deal, Jack mused.

"Meet their number," Jack told Robinson, "and we've got the loan."

"He's bluffing. He doesn't have one and a half over."

Jack's anxiety gave way to fear. "What am I supposed to do, Lord?" he whispered. "Three deals in a row. Why did this happen? What are you trying to tell me?"

His financial services and consulting business had seen good years, but the last six months had been a disaster.

Compton Atherton was struggling through one of the deepest valleys he had ever been in. In fact, it was one of the most intense trials he had ever experienced.

He agreed with Benjamin on the need to unite the believers for prayer, but he was tired. Ministry had taken its toll. His counseling left him emotionally drained. His marriage had suffered as his attention was directed to the problems in the congregation. He felt it was all give and no take. How many Sundays had he preached with conviction and sensed the move of the Holy Spirit, and then in the foyer at the end of the service have only a handful of parishioners even acknowledge the message? Most of them were so engulfed in their own problems they couldn't even say, "Good message, Pastor." He was as close to giving up as he had felt in all his years in ministry.

He had not wanted to come to Mountain Fire to begin with and had been trying intermittently to leave ever since he arrived. He felt concerned about his ability to persevere and stay the course. He considered moving back to Ohio to escape, to retreat. There was a loneliness in ministry that none of his family and friends ever seemed to understand.

Atherton was in a deep ravine that had affected his faith as well. He didn't feel lukewarm—he felt cold. He briefly considered asking the Lord to take him home. He had never felt that way before.

He wondered if it were these kinds of feelings that preceded a person going off the edge and entering a spiral of alcohol and homelessness. Maybe this is what preceded a person ending up on the streets, he thought.

With Tommy throwing the ball back each time, Nathanial Allan drilled five consecutive three pointers from twenty-five feet. Swish, five times in a row—no rim, no backboard, nothing but pure, clean net. On Tommy's last toss, Nathanial stormed the net and stuffed the ball with such force that the backboard and pole lurched forward, ricocheting Nathanial back and forth for a moment, as Tommy watched wide-eyed from the side of the court. Nathanial hung on the rim for several seconds before gently dropping to the ground.

"You should have been in the NBA, Dad!"

Nathanial smiled and put his hand on the boy's head. He ruffled Tommy's wavy blond hair as they walked toward the house, but his mind was racing, miles away. He was incredulous that Compton had accused him of "sheep stealing." He had never gone after anyone else's flock in all his years of ministry. He knew that, and God knew that. The Begay family came to Jesus Saves Pentecostal after making the rounds through Compton's church, the Spanish Assembly, Navajo Presbyterian, Faith Gospel Tabernacle, and Mission of the Cross. "The Circuit," as Nathanial called it. Unhappy with the music, unhappy with the pastor—any number of reasons brought the family through no less than five churches before ending up at Jesus Saves Pentecostal.

Nathanial left two messages at the church before deciding to call Compton at home. A young girl answered the phone. Nathanial identified himself, and the girl politely said, "One moment, please," but then returned saying that her father was busy with family devotions and couldn't come to the phone. Three calls, no response.

Nathanial sat at his desk and removed a piece of stationery from a brown wooden paper holder. In longhand he wrote a letter to Compton:

> Do you think you can willingly sin against a Christian brother and then ask the Lord to bless you? Considering your attitude, it would not surprise me if you were to lose additional members of your flock. You have placed the value of your family over mine by refusing my call. I would appreciate the opportunity to explain the background involving the Begay family coming to my church. My conscience is clear before the Lord. I have forgiven you, but you have hurt me deeply.
>
> Sincerely, and in the name of Jesus,
>
> Nathanial Allan

Nathanial was troubled. Benjamin had asked him to pray over the group, one by one, at the prayer assembly. Nathanial had agreed. So now he was supposed to approach Compton and pray for God's blessing upon him? After Compton had questioned his integrity and questioned his truthfulness? What are you doing, Lord? Nathanial wondered. Nathanial felt as stretched emotionally as the end of the basketball net he had disrupted earlier that evening.

Nathanial tossed and turned until midnight, finally getting up and retiring to the couch because he kept waking Amy up. His mind was still racing when he fell asleep, well into the wee hours of the morning.

She had been to every one of his wrestling matches since the tenth grade and had earnestly prayed for him during his time of drugs and alcohol. She had rejoiced when he committed himself to the kingship and lordship of Jesus Christ. When he proposed, she cried with joy. She worked while he attended seminary. She delighted in his internship. She supported Jacob unflinchingly in everything he did. When she became pregnant, she called all of her family and friends and expressed an almost inexpressible joy over the new life that God had blessed her with. There had never been a more happily married woman and never a happier mother. Janet loved her Lord, her husband, her child. And in one instant, the Lord took her home.

Why would the Lord bring me to this place just to lose my wife and child? Jacob thought.

He reflected on the prayer assembly. Janet would have been delighted to attend. She was a woman of prayer in the truest sense. He felt a sense of anguish over going alone. He carried a disappointment that weighed heavily on him. At times the disappointment turned to depression and finally to bitterness. Why would the Lord take his wife and daughter?

Robert Thompson was frustrated. Robert was a man who was always in control. He was prolific in ministry and in virtually every other aspect of his life. He thrived on a full schedule and took great satisfaction in knowing that every detail was in place. He would make goals to get up in the morning earlier—at four thirty or five o'clock—completing a list for the day, dividing it into hourly time frames. He managed a myriad of tasks and appointments with finely tuned administrative skills and seldom thought he had accomplished enough.

But now he felt overwhelmed. It was as though a full schedule of activities, beforehand always maintained with energy and drive, and balanced with a symmetry that he felt must be God-given, was now pressing in on him in ways he couldn't understand.

He was irritated with the freewill theology in Gary Smith's "Arminian" prayer at the last prayer meeting. He found himself feeling agitated when he thought of Nathanial's ministry among the East Indian motel owners and was irritated that Nathanial had requested his help at the soup kitchen before Christmas. Didn't he realize that Robert had his own church? Wasn't his schedule full enough?

He was upset with the ongoing self-righteousness he sensed in David Janssen.

Robert was intensely strong-willed. He prided himself in a resourceful ingenuity that yielded results in not only his ministry but in other endeavors as well. And now things were unraveling. God was sovereign. He would save with or without Gary's help.

Justin Randall reviewed the song list that he and Benjamin had collaborated on. They would begin the evening by singing a melodic rendition of 2 Chronicles 7:14. The lyrics to the entire song, with several repeats and a key change, were from the Scripture passage. Psalm 23 would follow—again, all Scripture. Jacob had composed the harmony, a slow, beautiful arrangement sung by the choir and assembly with an orchestra accompaniment. Jacob scanned the list: "God of Wonders," "All The Heavens," "A Mighty Fortress Is Our God," "Rock of Ages," "El Shaddai." Benjamin wanted a mix of contemporary music, traditional hymns of the faith, and several Messianic songs. A hymn in Spanish and a song in Navajo would be sung.

There would be soloists performing special music as well. Benjamin would sing "El Shaddai." Justin would play guitar and lead the choir in "The Sacrifice Lamb." The two had put together a wonderful song list, but it wasn't necessarily the list that he would have come up with. It irritated Justin that Benjamin took such an active role in the music. Jacob never did that, even with special services. He always allowed Justin to choose the music. Benjamin had insisted on input, saying there was a particular theme that needed to be honored.

Lyle Thorson, Benjamin's worship leader at Faith Gospel Tabernacle, would be in the choir. Lyle was an accomplished pianist and composer. He had written a number of praise songs for the Faith Gospel Tabernacle worship team. Justin had always felt a competitive spirit from Lyle. The two men were, without question, the most talented musicians and song leaders within all the Mountain Fire churches. Now, Justin was leading Lyle for the prayer assembly and he sensed Lyle's resentment. He shared his concern with Benjamin, who provided little empathy. "The Lord has put you in charge of the worship team, my friend. Run with it to Yeshua's glory." It wasn't that easy, Justin thought. It seemed strange that Benjamin would create a rivalry by choosing him over his own worship leader.

Justin was both a worship leader and a worshipper. He avoided conflict; he hated confrontation. He was not a personnel manager or a human resources director.

Emily Martha Bartholomew Smith, owner of the local Living Water Christian Bookstore and president of the Mountain Fire Right to Life chapter, was arguably the most beautiful woman that had ever set foot in this small community of thirty thousand— perhaps the most beautiful woman to have set foot in New Mexico, for that matter. And if Gary were polled, she was the most beautiful woman on the face of the planet. Emily displayed a fervor and passion for the Lord that was readily apparent to the diverse clientele who patronized her store. She was intense, outspoken, and direct.

"What will we do about the Pentecostal-Conservative problem?" Gary would often ask, particularly after hearing from a parishioner about something that had taken place at one of the Pentecostal churches. "Take it to the Lord," Emily would say—in a manner that displayed little patience for what she perceived as nothing more than childishness. "If they can't learn to get along with their brothers and sisters in Christ in this life, how are they going to get along in heaven? Do they think they'll have their own little corner away from everyone else?"

"There are doctrinal issues," Gary would say. "You can't discount all of our differences."

"There are certain nonnegotiable truths. But there are other things that won't be solved in this life. Isn't that what Benjamin always says?" Emily would reply. "How are your weekly meetings going? You seem to be hanging in there in spite of the differences."

"It's hard," Gary would reply. "Believe me, it's hard."

But it was more than hard. It was impossible, Gary thought. Why was he spending time on Benjamin's "pipe dream"—something that would never happen and, if it did, with only limited results?

In recent weeks, he had been struggling with feelings of resentment. He envied Benjamin. He envied the building, Faith Gospel Tabernacle, which Benjamin pastored in. He envied the size of the congregation Benjamin had, and he envied the vision that Benjamin often passionately expressed. He had paid his dues; he had ministered longer and harder, so he thought, than Benjamin or any of the other men, for that matter. At what point would his own ministry "break" and see the explosion of numbers he had hoped for? At what point would new converts stream down the aisles of his own church? Now he was laboring for flocks that were not his own.

Gary thought of all that he wanted to do in life: he especially wanted to travel—drive through the South and see the peanut fields in Georgia and the cotton fields of North Carolina, take the scenic Natchez Trace Highway, hike a portion of the Appalachian Trail, ride Eurail through twenty-two European countries. At times he felt that life was passing him by, that he would enter his twilight years having missed out on the opportunity to enjoy life. He could rarely get out of town because of the ministry, and on the occasions when an elder could fill the pulpit for him and the jail ministry was covered, the bookstore prevented Emily from leaving.

Gary took off his coat and slumped into his chair. He rested his elbow on the arm of the chair and laid his face in his hand. Emily Martha saw the look on her husband's face and knew instantly that something was very wrong. Emily walked down the hall to the bedroom and closed the door behind her. She then kneeled at the foot of the bed and began interceding for her husband and the pastoral group. She realized that a battle was going on. A prayer covering was needed.

Alexander recognized a problem with the men, and he was as close to experiencing despair as he could recall in seventy-one years. The group's fragility had been exposed in a manner that Alexander never would have imagined. He was angry—as angry as he was capable of feeling anyhow. He looked at his wife as she handed him a cup of coffee and then gently caressed his neck. "It doesn't make sense. Something happened in recent days. I don't understand it. It simply does not make sense!"

"What's wrong?"

"What's wrong is that Satan told Benjamin a lie—I'm not sure about what—and Benjamin bought it hook, line, and sinker. The prayer assembly is off. At least it's off as we know it."

Alexander walked into his study and looked at the built-in bookcase that covered two walls of the room. He glanced at the panoply of names: Bunyan, Chambers, Tozer, Lewis, Murray. Fifty years of learning and faithfully teaching the tenets of prayer and revival, and now his dream was dying. He was sure that he would never be this close again.

"What are you going to do, Alex?"

Alexander took his wife's hands in his and pulled her to himself. There was a pained expression in his eyes. "What else is there to do," he said, "but pray?"

Chapter Twelve

The attack on Benjamin one week before the prayer assembly had been orchestrated in the chambers of hell itself. Suddenly, the prayer assembly was off. The fury of the assault left Benjamin kneeling down at the foot of his bed, his body limply hunched over the end of the bed, looking as if he had been pummeled in a boxing ring and left helplessly on the ropes, unable to stand.

In spite of his recent concerns, he had planned on going through with it. He was even going to preach the message that he felt certain the Lord had placed on his heart. He would share the message with the people, the worship team would lead in song, the pastors and other Christian leaders would pray—beseeching God for the revival that they had been seeking—and then it would be up to God to move among the people. It would be the Holy Spirit that would convict of sin and manifest Himself in the assembly. Benjamin would be obedient and leave the rest to God.

And then the doubts began—slowly at first over the course of the morning but building in momentum by that evening to what Benjamin thought must resemble a nervous breakdown. He had never felt that level of emotional stress in his entire life—not after he became a Christian and was separated from his family, not during his five years in Israel.

First there were feelings of inadequacy; Benjamin lacked in love. How could someone who at times was so impatient lead the local body of Christ? He was intolerant of anyone who did not share the vision. He was judgmental of others' shortcomings and weaknesses. He would often think and sometimes say, "Confess your sin and move on. Don't stay there. There's work to be done!" This was not the attitude of a gentle, loving man. Were Benjamin the saint that God intended, he would be compassionate and understanding—not harsh and quick to dismiss.

And secondly, he was double-minded. How could the pastor of the largest church in Mountain Fire, and the leader under the Lord in calling the saints together for prayer, have been so easily swayed by feelings for a woman he hardly knew? For weeks his thoughts had been consumed by her. He had been like a man in an opium den who, in accepting the pipe, decided to recluse himself from life for a time by entering another world. Benjamin had literally been in a dreamlike state of consciousness as he struggled through the attraction. He should have rebuked the devil immediately in the name of Jesus and avoided the struggle. But then he had enjoyed the thoughts, so of course he didn't seek refuge right away.

Benjamin put his face in his hands and then pulled at his hair, his face grimacing in agony as he reflected on his plight. What an absolute worthless sinner I am, he thought.

Benjamin began to stand but then crumpled to the bed as if a sledgehammer had come down upon him. Satan had saved the best for last, and the words came screaming at Benjamin like an emergency siren in the middle of the night. "You have blood on your hands! You can't preach at this prayer assembly. You don't even belong in the auditorium! Do you think for a moment that God has changed His thoughts just for you? Doesn't the Bible say that Jesus Christ is the same yesterday, today, and forever? David was not allowed to build the temple. Do you think that you're a greater man of God than David? God's cherished servant who the Lord said was a man after His own heart? You're not a man of God at all. You're a hypocrite, Benjamin! You shouldn't be pastoring a church. If your congregation knew what you were about, you'd be living on the streets with those you claim to want to help. You're an utter failure. Quit now and save yourself a greater humiliation later."

Benjamin pushed himself up from the bed, off of the ropes as it were, and momentarily staggered. The din of the jeering crowd subsided. He took a deep breath, leaned on the mahogany dresser that stood against the wall, and looked at himself in the full-length closet mirror. It was over. His life was a lie. He would tell the group tomorrow that something had come up and he wouldn't be attending the prayer assembly. He would then determine the next step.

Benjamin could see the despairing look on their faces that afternoon as the men met for prayer. No one spoke. They were a week away from the prayer assembly, and the entire gathering was crumbling before his eyes. He felt his own desire and strength waning. Maybe now isn't the time, Benjamin thought.

Alexander understood what was happening and spoke softly. "We're not alone right now. The enemy is here in great magnitude. I can sense his evil presence trying to destroy what the Lord has built. But I sense an even greater presence and that is Jehovah Nissi—the Lord is our banner. Are we going to let the Evil One prevail, or will we stand victorious on the promises of God?" Alexander's voice rose and the men began to shout. Alexander began to pray. "O God! The enemy would thwart Your work, but greater is He that is in us than he that is in the world."

As Alexander was praying, the sweet presence of the Holy Spirit settled in the room, and a peace displaced the fear that had weighed so heavily on the men.

Jack Broholm spoke first. "I agree with Alexander. We've all studied great revivals. We know what precedes great moves of God. We understand what we're supposed to do. But along with that knowledge and understanding that God has granted us comes accountability. We'll have to answer to God if we turn back now."

David Janssen was next. "When Ron Stevens called me again, I was sure that he had gone to Milwaukee about the prayer assembly. I waited for him to tell me that if I participated, I'd be relieved of my post. But instead, he said, 'I've been praying about the community prayer meeting. You need to obey the Holy Spirit. I haven't said anything to anyone about the matter. God bless you and God be with you, David.'

"I will be there, Benjamin, as will a number of my parishioners. If word gets back to Milwaukee, then so be it—even if it costs me my pastorship."

"I've battled with the bitterness I feel over losing Janet," Jacob said. "As hard as it is for me to understand, the Lord has said to trust Him. I know that I'll see her again."

Compton Atherton reflected on the prior Sunday when one of the elders of the church had walked to the front of the sanctuary and said, "I feel led to pray for our pastor." The next day as Compton was walking through the house preparing for the day, he stopped and remembered the prayer on Sunday. He then began inquiring of the Lord and worshipping Him, saying, "Thank you, Lord Jesus, for Your deliverance." It suddenly occurred to Compton that he was doing what he routinely had done for years but what had been missing from his life for the past month during some of the darkest hours he could remember.

"I just came out of a period in my life when I seemed to worry about everything," Compton said softly. "I would never consider suicide, but I didn't want to live. I wanted to go home.

"The Lord spoke to me and impressed a verse upon my heart: 'casting all your care upon Him, for He cares for you.' I know the devil has done everything he can to hinder the prayer assembly. We must push ahead."

Robert Thompson then spoke. "A week ago I had the worst day of my life. I felt overwhelmed by pressure. I carried those feelings into our meeting this morning. I've felt resentment toward several of you. I beg your forgiveness. God be with us as we proceed to Friday night."

A final voice cried out, "We know what we're supposed to do. Why aren't we doing it?

"Benjamin, we are with you! Together we will serve the King for this city!"

Unbeknownst to the men, Benjamin had met with Alexander earlier that morning and shared his story.

"I was in an affiliate group of the Mossad for five years after college. I was in Israel for most of that time. Much of my work was administrative in nature, but for a time I was given the responsibility to monitor a man named Khalid who was part of the jihad. I killed him. When I was at the town hall meeting giving my speech I believe that I saw Abdul, who I now know to be a distant relative."

"How did he get here?"

"I don't know. But he's here legally. He's been in the country for ten years. He's been here for two.

"When Abdul yelled at me that night in Flagstaff, I felt a love for him that surprised me. God has been changing my heart.

"For years, I have always been reminded of that night in Gaza. Every stairwell, every concrete wall and crevice, dark nights, light bulbs burning out—I've asked the Lord to deliver me, but until my heart had changed, I was always reminded.

"Truly, I was at war. There was nothing else that I could have done. Khalid was linked to numerous suicide bombings. And yet, I have deep sorrow for having killed another man."

Benjamin paused and rubbed his fingers over his eyes momentarily. "Hafiz, his brother, was much younger. He was in training but did not have the status of Khalid. I'm glad I didn't have to kill him. They don't know that I'm here. It was twenty-five years ago."

Benjamin gazed intently at Alexander, looking for a reaction from his friend. "Now you know. We live in a complicated world. Oftentimes, our lives surprise us."

It was this five-year gap in Benjamin's life that he had never shared with the group. He knew that he had to tell the men.

Benjamin looked down. He couldn't face the group. He spoke softly, slowly. "I am a Messianic Jew. All of you know and understand that. I am also a Zionist. I believe in the statehood of Israel. I believe that the Jewish people still hold a special place in Yeshua's heart. I believe that there will be a great harvest of Jewish people in the days ahead."

The men nodded. Alexander replied, "Continue, son."

"Even after becoming a Christian, I hated Muslims. It

is only in recent years that God has changed my heart. I now can truly say that I love the Muslim people. Yeshua wills that none should perish, that all would come into a saving faith in Jesus. That includes not only those of European Anglo-Saxon descent but the Black man and the Navajo man. It includes the Jew. And it includes the Arab. Yeshua means that all races and nationalities are invited into His kingdom.

"I have a confession to tell you. I must tell you, regardless of the consequences. I am the worst of sinners, unworthy to lead the prayer assembly. There is blood on . . ."

David Janssen stood abruptly and faced the men. "I'm sorry, Benjamin. I have an appointment and I need to leave immediately. But I need to confess—God has been working in my heart. I'm prideful. I'm unclean. I pride myself in my knowledge of the Word. I ask all of you to forgive me." With that, David left.

Benjamin looked at Alexander. The story remained untold. Alexander shook his head slowly. "Not now," his eyes seemed to say.

Chapter Thirteen

The phone call just after midnight startled Benjamin, even though his apprehension about the prayer assembly had prevented him from falling asleep.

The voice on the other line was deep with a rich Middle Eastern accent. Benjamin had heard the voice before.

"Pastor Sharon?"

"Yes."

"We've only met once—long ago—but I've been attending your church in recent weeks. I want to thank you for your message on forgiveness."

"You're welcome. Perhaps we can meet at my office and talk more."

"I'm sorry to have called you so late. I felt we needed to talk."

"What is your name?"

There was a long silence before the man responded, "My name is Khalid."

The words came at Benjamin like an ice chest of cold

water suddenly being poured over his head. He had never forgotten the tone and inflection of the familiar voice and now the name was being spoken clearly through the phone. But it couldn't be. It was impossible. And yet, in an instant, Benjamin realized that this was not a physiological dream—nor was it a spiritual vision. The voice on the other end of the line must be part of a cruel hoax.

The man continued. "I felt that I needed to tell you my story in the event that we meet one day. And my hope is that we can meet. I have questions about your Yeshua that need answers. I also want to make clear the misconceptions you have about what happened. I want to clear up your apprehension about the past."

Benjamin now knew, although the stark reality of what was unfolding before him seemed to be affecting his equilibrium; he felt medicated, anesthetized. After twenty-five years! How could he be having this conversation all these years later?

"You said that we met once before. Do you mean at the church, after a service?"

"Pastor Sharon, you know where we met."

Benjamin steadied himself. He felt as if he might black out.

"Can you hold the line for a moment?" he managed. Benjamin held his hand over the receiver and glanced through the dimly lit dining room and study. "Dear God, what's happening here? What should I say to this man?"

Benjamin put the phone to his ear. "Khalid, are you there?"

"Yes, I am here, Pastor Sharon."

"Where have we met? Tell me."

"We met twenty-five years ago in a stairwell in Gaza. You thought you had killed me, but the bullet missed my heart. By the grace of God I lived. I was not the man you thought I was. Yes, I am Palestinian. Yes, I was part of the resistance movement. I was also in training to fight against the occupation."

Khalid paused for a moment before continuing in a steady, calm voice. "I know you believe that Palestine is the rightful homeland of the Jewish people. But at that time, I believed in the jihad. I believed we were fighting the occupiers."

Benjamin took a deep, long breath. "Why are you telling me this?"

"Because, as I said before, there are misconceptions that you hold to that I must make right. I was not a suicide bomber. I deplore the killing of innocent life—Jew or Palestinian. I was in training to be in the Palestinian army and to fight for my people in what I thought was a just war. Not to kill innocents. I was very young. I was very naïve. But the full indoctrination did not take a deep hold on me as it did others. As time went on I came to understand the brutality of what Hamas was doing to innocent people. I understood the lies and knew that Arafat was also oppressing our own people. I left the movement and shortly after was able to leave the country. My uncle is involved with the Indian jewelry trade. He helped secure my immigration papers. I was in Albuquerque for over twenty years. I became a citizen ten years ago. I've been in Mountain Fire now for less than a year."

Khalid stopped as if waiting for Benjamin to comment.

"I don't know what to say."

Khalid continued, "It's a remarkable story, I know. But it's a story I had to tell you. I'm not the man you thought I was."

"A Palestinian man tried to kill me a couple of months ago at a convenience store. Do you have information about that?"

"Yes, I know about it. He pointed a gun at you, but he could have pointed it at anyone. It was coincidental that you were there. It had nothing to do with us or our past."

"Who is he?"

"He's a relative to one of the jewelers. He came from Chicago, where he grew up. He's young. He's not involved with the struggle in any way. He's a drug addict."

"There were agents there."

"They had been following him. ISD linked him to a drug run."

"But the agents knew my name."

"Pastor Sharon," Khalid said quietly, "we all know your name. Your past is hidden from your Christian friends, but don't you know that all of the Arab community that is here from Jerusalem knows who you are? When you first came, fear swept through the area. They thought you were here as part of the struggle. Many believe that the church is a front to infiltrate the local Palestinian community."

"If they're not a part of the Palestinian cause, what are they afraid of?"

"They are not involved, but they have family that is involved. All of them know someone that is somehow connected. As a result of this knowledge, great paranoia exists. Surely, you understand. Those that believe your past is years behind you still hate you for your ideology. They hate Zionism and everything that it stands for. No one in the community represents that more than you. Not even the Christians. Remember, there are other issues too. Taxes, the drug trade, the same things that face the non-Arab community. Except with us, the fear is greater."

"You say that you've been attending Faith Gospel Tabernacle. Are you now a Christian?"

"I was sent to your church to monitor your activities. I came back the third and fourth times because I wanted to hear more. I know that you mean what you are saying to the people. I can tell that you love the people. That is the other reason I called—I believe the most important reason. I need to talk with someone. Someone who can give me answers. I've been reading the Bible. I sense a change coming over my life, but I feel as if I am in a personal battle more serious than the one I fought in Palestine.

"I have not made that commitment to your Yeshua. I cannot say that I am a Christian. I am concerned about my future if I choose that path. There is a price for me to pay if I make that decision. But I am also concerned about my eternal soul."

Benjamin was stunned. It would be impossible on such short notice, if ever, to compose adequate answers for the questions that were rapidly formulating in his mind.

"There can never be a price too great to keep you from Yeshua."

"I believe what you are saying, but I am very afraid. I need to talk to you, soon, in private—where no one will know. We have a mutual secret. I trust you."

They set up a time to meet, and Benjamin hung up the phone. He walked into the living room, dropped to his knees, lifted his hands to heaven, and began crying out praises to Yeshua. He remained in that position for an hour as praise came forth from his lips with such force and at such a decibel level that he thought surely the neighbors would be awakened and a knock on the front door would soon be coming.

And then he began confessing his sins, acknowledging his unworthiness, and pleading the blood of Jesus over every aspect of his life.

Another hour passed, and a peace came over Benjamin as the presence of the Lord filled the room. Benjamin leaned forward and lay prostrate on the floor, humbling himself before God and saying over and over in his inner man, "Thank You, Lord Jesus, Yeshua; thank You, Lord Jesus, Yeshua."

The morning sun emerged suddenly, shining brightly into the room, and Benjamin realized he had been laying prostrate for much of the night. He rose and went to his bedroom and fell into a deep sleep, still praising the Lord Jesus in his heart and soul.

Chapter Fourteen

That Friday night, an incredible scene began to unfold. The musicians and singers came first at about five o'clock, along with the sound men and the stage and light crew.

As the worship team began their dress rehearsal, others—primarily friends of someone on the worship team—filtered into the large auditorium and sat quietly as the songs resounded through the otherwise empty chamber.

And then an amazing thing began to happen. At about twenty minutes to seven o'clock, the arriving traffic heading to the auditorium converged on Monument Valley Boulevard, forming a solid stream of light in the dark January night.

They came from the north as far as Farmington, the south as far as Zuni, the east from Grants, and the west from Holbrook, Arizona.

At 7:00 p.m. the worship team began singing,

"Rock of Ages, cleft for me,
Let me hide myself in Thee;
Let the water and the blood,
From Thy wounded side which flowed,
Be of sin the double cure;
Save from wrath and make me pure."

They followed with "Exalt The Lord" and several other worshipful songs, and then Benjamin took the podium and began preaching. His text was from Esther chapter 4, "For such a time as this."

"Yeshua has brought us here tonight to worship Him. To put aside our differences and pray that He will find favor with us and move mightily in our midst."

As the people prayed and the assembly sang praises to the King, cries broke out through the auditorium. Gary Smith lay prostrate in front of the stage. Compton Atherton stood in the front row with both hands raised to heaven. Robert kneeled at his chair, thanking the Lord over and over.

Jacob danced in the front, much as he imagined King David would be doing if he were there. He imagined Janet and Barbara dancing with him before the Lord. Janet smiled at Jacob and kissed him. Barbara jumped into the outstretched arms of her father. Jacob held the little girl closely and spun her around. Jacob closed his eyes. The three of them were in heaven in a beautiful meadow of flowers. "Thank you, Lord Jesus," he whispered.

Nathanial walked the aisles, saying softly, "Jesus, Jesus, move among us, sweet Jesus."

David Janssen prayed boldly for a man from Nathanial's church. The man was sick with fever, but David rebuked the spirit of infirmity in the name of Jesus and commanded the man, in Jesus' name, to walk victoriously in health.

Justin faced the choir as the song "A Mighty Fortress Is Our God" began to play. The evening was long, but he wasn't tired. A glow came from the singers and musicians. Suddenly, there were angels singing in the choir. Tears streamed down Justin's face as the words "His kingdom is forever" resonated through the auditorium.

Jack Broholm walked to the hallway outside the auditorium doors and began laying his hands on, and praying for, those who stood with heads bowed and others who sat quietly on the floor. "Bless you in the name of Jesus. The Lord Jesus bless you."

Alexander could not remember a more joyful time in his life. As the evening progressed, and the Spirit of God fell gently yet powerfully on the congregation, Alexander wondered if his life was ending. Perhaps God was now going to take him home. Tonight he was experiencing everything he had wanted to see for the last fifty years. It had taken half a century, but God was faithful. Tonight, in his lifetime, Alexander was seeing the beginnings of revival. A revival not confined to one church but a revival that was inclusive of the entire local body of Christ.

When the cries and weeping finally subsided,

Benjamin approached the podium. "The Lord has placed on my heart a burden for some of you who don't know Yeshua as the Christ and Lord and Savior. Don't neglect the day of His visitation. You may not have this chance again. If you need Yeshua, Jesus, I want you to come forward right now and kneel at this altar and surrender your life to Him. Come right now. The Spirit of God is present. Don't refuse Him. He longs to take up residence in your life. He will indwell your heart and lead you into righteousness. Yeshua loves you more than you can ever know. Come now!"

One hundred men and women, young and old, streamed down the aisles of the auditorium and knelt at the foot of the platform. A man from the hallway cried out, "I need Jesus."

Benjamin continued. "I'm going to pray aloud. If you sincerely believe what I'm saying, I want you to repeat each line with me: Great and merciful God. Creator of the universe. I confess that I am a sinner. Thank You for sending Yeshua, Jesus, to die for me. I accept Your sacrifice on the cross. Thank You, Jesus, for dying for me. Come into my heart, Lord Jesus. Fill me with the Holy Spirit. Change my heart, O God. Make me the person You want me to be. In Jesus' name. Amen."

Benjamin left the stage and walked down the steps to the front where the people were kneeling. He began praying over them, "Jehovah-shammah, the Lord is present. Thank You for being with us tonight. You are a mighty warrior. You alone change lives. You alone are worthy of our praise. Rain Your Spirit upon these people, dear God."

At the same moment Benjamin heard a voice calling him by name, he caught a glimpse of a man out of the corner of his eye. The man was on his knees toward the front of the stage, off to the side by himself. Benjamin knelt down and put his arm around his shoulder. "Did you pray with me? Did you mean it?"

"Yes," Khalid whispered. "When I called last night, I was at a point of desperation. At one time I hated you, but you've saved my life. No, your Yeshua has saved my life."

"I will be there for you. We can meet anytime. It will be hard, but Yeshua will never let you down."

"I believe you."

Benjamin stood up. The men clasped hands and held them together for what seemed to be an eternity. "I will tell you one day how much your call meant to me," Benjamin said. "Shalom, my friend."

After closing his message and invitation with a prayer, Benjamin spoke again. "Something great and powerful has begun here this evening. Don't let what God is doing tonight end in this auditorium. Pastors, I encourage you to become part of a small group that meets regularly for prayer. Pray about the size of your group. It should be small enough for the members to develop bonds and establish an intimacy with each other. But, along with your congregations, it should be large enough to make a difference in your community. Seven is the ideal num-ber—a number divine in its attributes and characteristics."

Chapter Fifteen

The battle will ebb and flow in accordance with the repentance and prayers of God's people.

"I'm referring to a concentrated, ground-floor, grassroots effort that sweeps through neighborhoods, villages, towns, cities, counties, states, and countries. One that results in an evangelism tidal wave such as the world has never known, nor will ever know again." Alexander paused.

A student cried out, "Who will lead this charge, Professor?"

Alexander smiled, "The Lord of Hosts Himself. Jesus. The Lion of the Tribe of Judah, the King of Glory. And under the Lord, men like Benjamin Sharon; there will be many others—all submitted to the lordship and kingship of Jesus."

"And men like Alexander Joseph," the student replied.

Alexander closed his eyes and lifted his head toward heaven, and a brightness overtook his countenance as the sun glistened through the window, transforming his grandfatherly face into a youthful glow the student imagined to be of a prophet.

Alexander bowed his head before looking once again to heaven and saying, "Even so, come, Lord Jesus."

That afternoon, Benjamin pulled his Suburban into the parking lot of the college, got out, and began walking toward the starting point of his familiar running path when he spotted Alexander leaving his classroom.

The men approached one another and momentarily embraced. "Shalom aleichem," Benjamin said.

Alexander smiled, "And peace to you, my friend."

The two spoke very little; they knew. God had moved in a powerful way.

Alexander got in his car and began the drive home.

The freshly fallen snow from the night before rested gracefully on the piñon and juniper trees, sparkling in the afternoon sun as Benjamin headed east of the college on his twelve-mile run, singing softly,

"Oh, the blood of Jesus.
Oh, the blood of Jesus.
Oh, the blood of Jesus.
It washes white as snow."

The End

Epilogue

To: The Faculty and Student Body of Prince of Peace Presbyterian, Grand Rapids, Michigan. Subject: "Revival" – For publication in the March issue of *The Flaming Sword – Words for Today*.

To the Christian throughout the church age, the word *revival* has had several meanings. In contemporary times, the word is oftentimes associated with "tent revival" or "camp revival" or, sometimes, "special revival services"—all meant to describe a setting where the preaching, teaching of God's Word, and singing of His goodness will carry forth in a prolonged manner, allowing for His people to experience a "reviving," living anew with a fresh touch in their lives from God.

To the historic church through the ages, the word *revival* represented a period of broad reflection and insight, always consummating in a change in the condition of the body of Christ from coldness to fervent hearts, warm and ablaze for the Saviour.

To the heathen nations under God's judgment, the condition of revival followed a state of fear and subsequent repentance, allowing the people a reprieve from the wrath of God, an opportunity to avoid certain destruction.

In Western society of the twenty-first century, revival has sometimes come to signify a place or venue where God's presence is manifest in a special and powerful way.

One pastor has said that revival is when the best of God's people get better.

For me, the word *revival* has come to represent the answer to one of the most important questions of the day. And that is, "In a world churning rapidly into the new millennium, what can America ill afford to do without?" Answer: True heartfelt revival among those who profess the lordship of Jesus Christ.

Throughout the ages, before the birth of Christ, our King, and two thousand years after His death and resurrection, one thing stands clear: when God's people pray, earnestly and diligently seeking His face for His glory, His presence is made known in the land.

Second Chronicles 7:14 states, "If my people, which are called by my name, shall humble themselves, and pray, and seek my face, and turn from their wicked ways; then will I hear from heaven, and will forgive their sin, and will heal their land."

I submit this essay with great joy as I now at this moment, with enthusiasm I can scarcely contain, share with you that revival indeed has come to Mountain Fire, New Mexico. May the Lord Jesus bless you wonderfully!

Respectfully,

Alexander Joseph

In the year of our Lord 2006

About the Author

R. A. Stokes lived in western New Mexico for close to thirteen years. For a number of those years, he was privileged to have a ministry involving prayer and evangelism. Mr. Stokes desires, in these last days before the Lord's return, to see the body of Christ—all those who are washed in the blood of Jesus—seek God's face for a mighty move of the Holy Spirit, as Christians throughout the world await that awesome day of the Lord, the return of our great Savior, Lord, and King, Jesus Christ!

Mr. Stokes believes that as God's people pray, revival and transformation can take place in cities across the land. *The Nehemiah Project* will be an encouragement to prayer intercessors and other ministers of the gospel, whether pastor, layman, teacher, or worship team member.

* 9 7 9 8 9 8 7 2 4 5 9 0 3 *